A HUNDRED RENEGADE BRAVES—
AND ONE BRAVE WOMAN...

Windy Mandalian's face was taut when he reined in beside Lt. Fitzgerald.

"Found him, Lieutenant."

"Wraps-Up-His-Tail?"

"None other. Four miles south by west."

"Four miles off?" Fitzgerald looked to the darkening skies. "We'll ride to high ground and make night camp. No smoke, no talking. I want to hit them at first light."

"That's the best way," Mandalian said. "But we've got us a small problem, Lieutenant. They outnumber us three to one...."

EASY COMPANY

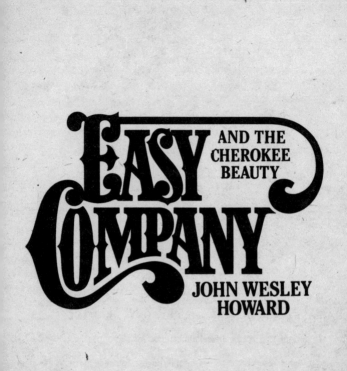

EASY COMPANY

AND THE CHEROKEE BEAUTY

JOHN WESLEY HOWARD

A JOVE BOOK

EASY COMPANY AND THE CHEROKEE BEAUTY

First Jove edition published March 1982

First printing

Printed in the United States of America

Jove books are published by Jove Publications, Inc., 200 Madison Avenue, New York, N.Y. 10016

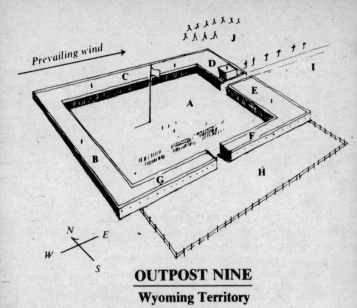

Prevailing wind

J

D

I

C

E

A

F

B

G

H

N
E
W
S

OUTPOST NINE
Wyoming Territory
KEY

A. Parade and flagstaff

B. Officers' quarters ("officers' country")

C. Enlisted men's quarters: barracks, day room, and mess

D. Kitchen, quartermaster supplies, ordnance shop, guardhouse

E. Suttler's store and other shops, tack room, and smithy

F. Stables

G. Quarters for dependents and guests; communal kitchen

H. Paddock

I. Road and telegraph line to regimental headquarters

J. Indian camp occupied by transient "friendlies"

INTERIOR   OUTSIDE

OUTPOST NUMBER NINE
(DETAIL)

Outpost Number Nine is a typical High Plains military outpost of the days following the Battle of the Little Big Horn, and is the home of Easy Company. It is not a "fort"; an official fort is the headquarters of a regiment. However, it resembles a fort in its construction.

The birdseye view shows the general layout and orientation of Outpost Number Nine; features are explained in the Key.

The detail shows a cross-section through the outpost's double walls, which ingeniously combine the functions of fortification and shelter.

The walls are constructed of sod, dug from the prairie on which Outpost Number Nine stands, and are sturdy enough to withstand an assault by anything less than artillery. The roof is of log beams covered by planking, tarpaper, and a top layer of sod. It also provides a parapet from which the outpost's defenders can fire down on an attacking force.

one _____

The wind was hard out of the north. The long grass
trembled before it. There was new spring grass now, after
the recent rains, showing brilliant green in patches inter-
spersed with the older, brown grass, much of which had
been flattened by weather and buffalo. The wind clutched
at an old broken cottonwood and throttled it. A dust devil,
picked up on a barren knoll, was swept across the plains
and dropped nearly in front of Lieutenant Fitzgerald's
chunky, deep-chested bay.

He closed his eyes tightly against the dust. Then he wiped
the sweat from his forehead and turned in the saddle to study
the rest of his detachment briefly. The sun was in their eyes,
and it was still a hot sun, and the men rode with their hats
low, squinting into the yellow heat of the day.

He was aware suddenly of Gus Olsen moving up beside
him. The platoon sergeant wore an expression of concern
mixed with his usual affability.

"Got scouts coming in, Lieutenant," Olsen said, and
Fitzgerald's eyes followed the stubby pointing finger to the
north, where Windy Mandalian's appaloosa stood out
against the dry grass plains. Behind Windy and slightly to
the west was Joseph Hatchet, the Delaware scout. Neither
man was trying to make time. They alternately walked and

1

loped their ponies toward the detachment, which plodded westward, enveloped in yellow dust clouds of its own making.

"Looks like they've got nothing to report," Fitzgerald said, more to himself than to Olsen.

"Nothin' urgent," Gus agreed.

Fitzgerald glanced again at the sun, and frowned. They were a good fifteen miles out, and he was beginning to grow uneasy about this expedition. They were far enough from Outpost Number Nine to be cut off if that damned Wraps-Up-His-Tail had as many warriors as the "moccasin telegraph" had reported.

"Keep your eyes open for a campsite, Sergeant," Fitzgerald said. "Darkness will be coming up on us real quick."

Olsen nodded and let his horse fall back behind the lieutenant's. Windy was nearly to the point of the column now, Hatchet still a quarter of a mile off.

Fitzgerald took a deep drink from his canteen and sighed, watching Windy trail in. Wraps-Up-His-Tail was out here somewhere. The Crow had been spotted by Chase, one of Windy's informants, and the word passed on by runner. He hadn't had time to break camp, or at least Fitzgerald doubted it. The moccasin telegraph moved quickly. When Matt Carrol of the Diamond D bull trains was asked to ride from General Crook's headquarters on the Rosebud to carry news of the Little Big Horn disaster north to Fort Keogh, a trip that took the hard-riding Carrol three days, he found out that the Indians around the fort had gotten news of the battle the day before he arrived.

"You're coming in damn slow these days," Fitzgerald told Windy as the scout pulled in behind him. Windy shook his head and spat a stream of tobacco juice, wiping his lips with his sleeve.

"Yes," Windy drawled, "and if you see me comin' in quick, you'd best have these boys unlimber their guns."

"You didn't see anything?" He looked at Hatchet. The Delaware apparently had nothing to report, either.

"No sign of Mr. Lo," Windy answered. He took off his

2

flop hat and wiped back his long, thinning hair. "Old Chase, he knew exactly where they was. But this area is crisscrossed by draws and coulees, Lieutenant. Now an Indian like Chase, he's lived here all his life and he knows where the second buffalo wallow up the coulee by the big trees is, could find it on a dark night in his sleep. Me, I've a good notion where the damned Crow is supposed to be, but it'll take a little scouting."

"Just so we find him before he gets too eager to show his stuff."

Windy nodded agreement and swung out to talk to Joseph Hatchet. The Delaware had seen nothing, but his pony had pulled up lame.

Fitzgerald watched the endless prairie, where in the far distance, the Rockies showed as a low, nearly purple line against the dun brown of the horizon, and he silently cursed. He could have been in Kansas City. They were due for furlough, all of them.

Captain Conway was gone to Denver to spend some time in a soft bed with Flora, and with any luck they would eventually get a summer relief officer to Outpost Number Nine, but in the meantime it was grinding. The outpost was habitually undermanned, and now the only officers were Taylor, Kincaid, and Fitzgerald, all of them itching for furlough.

"I think we might want to camp on that knoll, Lieutenant," Sergeant Olsen said. Fitzgerald hadn't even noticed the big man riding up beside him. He glanced at the low knoll where a half-dozen big oaks stood, shuddering in the wind, then turned to look at his detachment; the men were dusty, weary, purpled by the sundown light.

"All right," he agreed. "Post a double guard, Sergeant."

"I was intendin' to, sir," Olsen answered. "What about a fire?"

"Only until dark. I don't suppose a fire could show any farther than this dust we're kicking up."

They made camp beneath the oaks, watching the crimson fire of the sun extinguish itself while coffee boiled. The

3

bedrolls were already rolled out, and several soldiers, exhausted by the day in the saddle beneath the hot sun, were already snoring.

The night guards ate first and were given coffee, then they spread out, filtering through the shadows toward their assigned posts.

At full dark, Olsen ordered dirt thrown onto the fire, and that triggered a lot of grumbling. Dillson was the loudest complainer, as he was the loudest complainer about everything from the red ants on the ground beneath the oaks to the strength of the coffee.

"If the scouts can't find no Injuns, then they're damn sure too far off to see a fire."

"Not at night, Dillson," Gus Olsen told him. "Use your head."

"It's bullshit," Dillson muttered, leaning back against the rough trunk of an oak. "Matter of fact, this is the most bullshit outfit I've ever been hooked up with."

Reb McBride glanced up from his coffee and said without a smile, "It sure as hell is since you showed up, Dillson."

Olsen sighed and walked away. There was no way short of beating Dillson to death to shut him up. Gus knew, he had tried. So had Ben Cohen, and when Cohen couldn't handle a man, the man was a lost cause.

Not that he wasn't a good soldier; Dillson was—or could have been. But he had been in the artillery before, and hated everything that wasn't artillery. If they'd let him, Dillson would be walking around in those redleg pants he'd brought with him.

Cohen was trying to get him back to artillery, but it wasn't easy. Apparently, Dillson hadn't been too well loved even there. Dillson watched Olsen walk away to sit beside the now-cold fire on a rotten log.

"Still bullshit," Dillson mumbled.

"I don't want to risk my hide on it," Reb told him. "Besides, it's an order. Don't you artillery boys take orders?"

"Damn right we do," Dillson flared up. "But in artillery you've got good noncoms, good officers."

"Gus Olsen is one of the best there is," Rafferty said from behind his forward-tilted hat.

"Bullshit."

They sat there in silence for a while, the only sounds the humming of mouse-sized mosquitoes, the occasional slap of a hand against someone's neck in retaliation.

"Who the hell is this Wraps-Up-His-Tail anyway?" Dillson asked.

"Just a hostile," Rafferty said, his voice broken by a yawn. "Damned renegade Crow is what he is."

"Crow!" Dillson snorted. "They worried about a Crow gettin' these Cheyenne and Plains Sioux together?" He laughed, his mouth hanging open stupidly. Dillson was an ox of a man, almighty thick through the chest and shoulders. The bulk of his body was sheathed in extra meat, and even his face was excessively heavy, with bulldog pouches on his cheeks.

"He's got big medicine," Reb McBride said, rolling over onto his side, his head propped up on his hand. "Way Windy heard it from Chase, the man's claimin' he can make himself invisible."

"Why, he could be out there right now!" Dillson said with mock horror. Then he laughed again. "Them Injuns'll swallow anything, won't they?"

"They're desperate, I reckon," Reb said. "A white man swallows just as much garbage. But a man comes up to these men and tells 'em he can defeat the army—why, there's always a few ready to give it a try."

"I heard," Rafferty put in, "that Wraps-Up-His-Tail is sayin' he can kill a man with a knife at a mile just by pointing it at him. It's big medicine, and there's always a few malcontents, braves who've been run off from their own tribes, kids wanting to earn their feathers to follow a medicine man who promises to make 'em strong."

For Dillson, who had asked the question in the first place, the explanation was too long. He was already snoring. The question had arisen from his complaining, but he really had no interest in the Crow medicine man; when it was time to fight, he would fight. Now it was time to sleep, and he did that as greedily and noisily as he did everything else, his great slack jaws quivering as he rumbled a snore.

"Listen to that," Rafferty said with a grimace.

"Yeah," Reb responded. "Thank God he's a likable son of a bitch otherwise."

"You know, Reb, one of us could just walk over there and slit his damned throat for him. Blame it on the hostiles."

"Could," Reb agreed. "But hell, he probably *bleeds* noisy."

Rafferty chuckled and rolled up in his blankets, and Reb did the same, tugging his blanket up around his ears.

They moved out at first light, riding westward in a picket line, with Windy Mandalian and Joseph Hatchet a good mile ahead. There was more new grass as they moved toward the mountains, and a good-sized herd of buffalo grazing placidly to the south. Fitzgerald felt better without the dust, although he still had only a slender hope of coming up unseen on Wraps-Up-His-Tail.

They saw nothing through the long morning except a pair of rail-thin, scavenging wolves working over a buffalo carcass. The wolves loped off as the squad approached, watched with yellow eyes from the long grass, and circled back as they passed.

They reached Tankford Coulee just before two o'clock, and the soldiers funneled down through a sandy cut into the bottom, which was heavy with budding cottonwood and willow.

There was enough water there for the horses, so Fitzgerald halted them there. It was hot even in the shade. Sweat trickled down his neck. His uniform, which had been fresh upon leaving Number Nine, was white with sweat.

He let his bay drink its fill, and his thoughts inevitably drifted to Kansas City. First the captain would have to get back, but he was due. Then it was Kincaid's turn for furlough—say a month, then. A month in a real hotel bed with silk sheets, cognac, and women in satin ball gowns...

His head came up sharply with the shout, and he yanked his startled bay's head around. The Indian had been lying

6

low in the willows, and now he had decided to make his break for it.

Fitzgerald saw a flash of color on the man's face, the blurred coloring of his roan through the screen of willow. Then the rider swung his pony up the sandy banks of the wash and achieved the flats in a flurry of sand.

"Rafferty! Dillson!" He swung his arm toward the two mounted men nearest him, and they spurred their horses into a run.

Rafferty had seen the Indian nearly at the moment Lieutenant Fitzgerald did, but he was frozen into immobility. When he did move, it was ineffectually, starting his pony, then stopping to grab at his Springfield.

But when Fitzgerald waved his arm, Rafferty heeled his bay forward. He had been told before that he was quicker at following orders than when thinking for himself. Maybe it was true.

Now he splashed his horse across the yard-wide stream and urged him up the sandy bluffs, feeling his horse sink nearly to its haunches as he spurred upward.

The horse scrambled for purchase and then was up, running on the broad flat plains. Rafferty glanced over his shoulder to see Dillson coming up quickly. The big man rode stiff-backed in the saddle, which might have struck Rafferty as funny at another time.

Now his attention was only on the Indian pony ahead of him, and the brave who rode low across its withers. It was a dead-out horse race, and Rafferty knew the bigger army horses would run down the mustang pony. He only hoped, with fleeting panic, that the Indian wasn't leading them into a trap.

He crossed his right hand and drew his Schofield Smith & Wesson, which was holstered on his left side, butt forward, and fired a shot well over the Indian's head, hoping that it might pull him up.

The Indian didn't even look back, which told Rafferty that the man had something to run from. A friendly, perhaps startled by the soldiers, might have taken off. Might have, but he damn sure would have stopped rather than get shot.

The dust plumed out behind Rafferty's horse. The bay was running well, taking long, ground-devouring strides, despite the long trail.

He was closing the gap between himself and the fugitive. Glancing back, Rafferty could see that Dillson was keeping pace, though he was eating a lot of dust.

The Indian was there, and then he wasn't, and Rafferty guided his pony to one side, still at a dead run, knowing the Indian had found a wash and might just leap off his pony's back and fight.

He intended to come up on the wash just a little north of where he was expected to appear. Rafferty hoped Dillson had taken a clue from him and swerved off to the south, but the big man was still in his dust. Rafferty waved a hand, motioning Dillson away. The big man, misunderstanding, slowed his horse instead, and Rafferty cursed.

"Dumb son of a bitch!"

Dillson had never wanted to sit around jawing with the men, and as a result he had learned nothing since arriving at Number Nine. Rafferty cursed his luck for drawing Dillson on this. Reb, Malone, Stretch, or any of them would have swung their horses south, and the result would be that the Indian would be caught between the searchers.

Rafferty saw the wash open up suddenly before him. Steep-walled, fifty feet deep, clotted with cottonwoods and contending brush, it offered what the Indian had been looking for: concealment.

Rafferty slid his bay down the bank, drawing up at the bottom in the dust of his own making, listening to the silence. Cicadas and mosquitoes hummed in the willow brush. Upstream a ways, bullfrogs grumped in the reeds. Rafferty looked back, saw no sign of Dillson, and dismounted, lifting his Springfield from the spider on his saddle.

He moved into the brush, pausing to listen every few steps. It was warm in the wash, shielded from the breeze as he was. He heard no telling sound, saw no movement or patch of color.

He wove through the brush-clotted wash, hands cramped around his Springfield, boots swishing through the sand underfoot. He started a cottontail to running, and his rifle swung that way automatically. Swallowing a tense curse, Rafferty wiped the salt sweat from his eyes and walked on, moving now to a sort of bench from which he had a view of the bottoms. Dillson never did show; Rafferty figured the man was watching to make sure the Indian did not break out onto the flats again.

It was unlikely that the brave would try that, Rafferty thought. He had cover in the wash, and he would know the main body of soldiers would be arriving shortly. Knowing that, the Indian would stick to the bottoms and he would move soon. North or south? That was the only question. Rafferty's eyes scanned the wash. He could see nothing yet, all the way to the big westward bend a half-mile off, and if the Indian had gotten that far, he was a magician. The brush was heavy, and that pony would have to make noise crashing through it.

Rafferty's tongue was dry. His chest was soaked with perspiration, and his shirt clung to it. He squatted down himself, holding his own silence, leaving it to the Indian to make his move.

And then he was there. Bursting out of the willows, his pony leaping over a dead tree, the Indian heeled his paint directly toward Rafferty. Rafferty saw the Indian's arms come up, saw the rifle in his hands, and he threw himself to one side, hearing the explosion, the muffled impact of the bullet into the sand near his head.

A second shot followed on the heels of the first. Still the Indian charged at Rafferty, and Rafferty brought his Springfield around. He could see the paint on the warrior's face clearly: green and yellow on one side of his face. He could even see that the man's nose had once been broken. He heard the pounding of the pony's hoofs, the hard breathing of the wild-eyed horse, and then a shot exploded behind and above him, and he flinched reflexively.

The smear of crimson appeared on the Indian's bare chest, and the horse turned sharply away from Rafferty, who was braced, prepared to dive headlong to one side. The pony heeled around, spraying a shower of dust at Rafferty, and the Indian tumbled from its back.

The body rolled head over heels once, and then stopped dead next to Rafferty as the bucking paint pony lunged downstream through the brush.

Rafferty sat there for a moment, his heart pounding. Not five feet away the Indian lay, faceup. His chest was torn open by a big .45-70 bullet. His heart gave one convulsive leap and then stopped, the blood leaking out to stain the white sand. The Indian, his expression savage even in death, stared into the sun with open, angry eyes.

Rafferty heard a noise behind him and spun around, but it was only Dillson. The big man slid down the bluff in a small avalanche of sand and rocks, landing on his rump beside Rafferty.

Dillson was grinning, rifle held high, and he got to his feet, poking the Indian with a boot toe.

"Saved your ass, I reckon!" he said triumphantly.

"I guess you did," Rafferty had to admit. He too was studying the dead brave. A shadow crossed his face and he glanced up now to see a line of horses against the sky.

"Dead?" Lieutenant Fitzgerald called down.

"Yes, sir!" Rafferty called back, and he heard Fitzgerald breathe a slow, fluent curse. Dillson had his hat off, mopping his forehead.

A line was thrown down, and Rafferty looped the rope under the dead warrior's armpits, then retrieved his bay and heeled it, stumbling, up the precipitous slope. He dismounted and watched as the Indian was dragged up and over.

Windy slid from his appy's saddle and strode over, going to his haunches to study the bloody body. Lieutenant Fitzgerald remained on his horse as Windy stood and announced, "Oglala Sioux." He shook his head. "Ain't a whole lot more to be learned from a dead man, Lieutenant."

"No." Fitzgerald's mouth was compressed into a straight, harsh line. "Damn," he breathed. He had wanted the man alive.

Dillson was just clambering up from out of the gulley, a grin on his bulldog face.

"Rafferty!" the lieutenant shouted, and Rafferty turned that way. "Come here. You too, Dillson."

The big man spat and walked to where Fitzgerald waited, still on horseback. "What happened, Dillson? You know I wanted that man alive."

Dillson's face went beet red and he sputtered before answering: "Sir, he was about to ride Rafferty here down. He had cut his dogs loose and I had to send mine out, else watch Rafferty take it."

"Is that right, Rafferty?" Fitzgerald asked.

"That's the way it was, Lieutenant. That Sioux was just about to bury me."

"All right." Fitzgerald looked away, studying the distances for a moment. The wind flattened the cheat grass, turning it silver. A lone crow circled against a high, brilliant sky.

It was important to have this Sioux runner alive, but he knew that Dillson had no real choice in it. Still, the big man could have tried to drop the Indian's pony, tried to wound him. That shot was dead center.

"That's all, boys," Fitzgerald said. He snapped a half-salute and turned his bay.

"That son of a bitch," Dillson muttered.

"It's just that he wanted the man alive," Rafferty said with a shrug.

Dillson blinked with incomprehension. "And you dead?"

"That's not what he meant," Rafferty told him.

"I save your butt, and you side with him against me!"

"I'm siding with no one, Dillson. I know you pulled me out of the fire back there. I'm just telling you that Fitzgerald didn't mean anything personal by what he said. He's just mad that the thing blew up in our faces."

"He just wanted to walk on somebody," Dillson said angrily. His eyes shuttled to where Fitzgerald, dismounted, stood talking to Windy Mandalian. "Anybody. He's one of them officers that's got to ride somebody, got to prove something to his men."

11

"Fitzgerald?" Rafferty laughed out loud. Dillson regarded him with a scowl, his dark eyes narrow and hard.

"All of 'em," Dillson said. He spat and turned sulkily toward his horse, still grumbling to himself.

Windy Mandalian had been cogitating, and when the lieutenant swung down beside him, the scout told him what he thought.

"I think this Sioux was a renegade, sir. He's got no reason to be roamin' around this far west by his lonesome, otherwise. I also think I know where he was going when we came up on him."

"Wraps-Up-His-Tail?"

"Yes, sir. Where else? The Crow's the only one we know of who's camped hereabouts. Now I figure this Oglala was either goin' to or comin' from Wraps-Up-His-Tail's camp. Could be I'm wrong, of course, but we got no other leads. If me and old Hatchet take a wide swing back toward the other coulee, we'll likely cut his sign, and while there's still good light, we can track him back and see where he's come from.

"If that don't wash," Mandalian continued, "we'll come back this direction and try to get a line on where he was goin'. The way I see it, one end or t'other will be Wraps-Up-His-Tail's camp."

Fitzgerald couldn't fault the logic of it, and as Mandalian had reminded him, they had no other leads. He sent Windy and Hatchet on back then, glancing at the sun, which was already midway through its descending arc.

Fitzgerald took the opportunity to send a party down into the wash to fill the canteens, which hadn't been filled at the coulee. His eyes settled then on the dusty, blood-caked form of the Sioux, and he called Sergeant Olsen over.

"We need a burial detail, Sergeant."

"Yes, sir." Gus looked at the body, noticing the blue-bottle flies that had already gathered, tracking across the dead man's eyes. "I'll see to it."

"Rafferty and Dillson," Fitzgerald said, not looking at Olsen directly.

"Sir?"

"I want Rafferty and Dillson to bury the man. It's their fault he's lying here."

"Yes, sir," Olsen answered, saluting smartly. It wasn't punishment, exactly, but it would be a reminder to Dillson and Rafferty. Although Dillson was sure to blow his top over this. Gus found the two men sitting in the shade of their horses, drinking from their canteens.

"What's up, Gus?" Rafferty asked.

"Him." He nodded at the corpse. "Lieutenant wants you men to bury him."

"Fuck him," Dillson snarled.

"You better hold it down," Olsen warned him sharply.

"Or what?" he asked challengingly.

"You know damned well what," Olsen said. "This is an order, Dillson. Bury that damned Indian."

Dillson came to his feet heavily, his face livid. "I chased him. I caught him. I shot him before he could kill Rafferty! Now, as thanks, I get to bury the fuckin' savage."

"That's right. Fitzgerald figures he's your responsibility, I guess."

Dillson's jaw was tight. The big man was ready to come unhinged. "I ought to tear him out of that uniform and break his goddamned face for him," he growled.

Reb McBride had wandered over, drawn by the sounds of arguing voices. What he saw was a man at the frayed end of his self-control, standing in front of a wooden Gus Olsen, his dark eyes fixed on Lieutenant Fitzgerald. Reb stepped in, trying to defuse it.

"I'll give you a hand, Dillson. Hell, ain't this the army for you? Chickenshit outfit, ain't it?" He pulled the shovel from Dillson's pack and took the big man's arm, grinning and jabbering, but Dillson shook him off.

Olsen had walked away, glancing over his shoulder. Rafferty hissed, "Dammit, Dillson. You don't talk like that about an officer!"

"Talk ain't all I'll do."

"Yeah, and then they'll do *you*. Up against the wall, bang-bang."

"I don't give a shit, Rafferty."

13

"You will, you will."

"Hit an officer and likely they'll just gun you down here to save you the misery," Reb put in. He could no longer hold the smile on his face. He put his arm on Dillson's shoulder, felt the knot of tensed muscles there, and said gently, "Come on. It's a soldier's life. You know that. Just more bullshit."

"I'm gonna get that son of a bitch," Dillson promised. His eyes lingered on Fitzgerald awhile longer, then he turned angrily away, yanking the shovel out of Reb's hand. Rafferty stood beside the bugler, watching Dillson stalk heavily toward the dead Sioux.

"Thanks, Reb," Rafferty said. His face was pale beneath the coating of yellow dust.

"It's nothin'. Hell of it is, I did it for a man I'd just as soon see shot."

"You and me both," Rafferty agreed, but he knew Reb only half meant it. Dillson was a pain in the butt, but a man sticks up for his partners. Even a redleg. Rafferty snatched up his own shovel and walked off to where Dillson, in a cloud of dust, was furiously shoveling dirt.

Reb watched them both a minute, then shook his head and walked to his own horse. Stretch Dobbs handed him his reins.

"What's that?" Stretch wanted to know.

"A man headin' for disaster just as fast as he can go," Reb answered.

They drifted slowly westward half an hour later, leaving the Sioux to his gods. The sun was in their eyes; their horses cast long, crooked shadows behind them. They hadn't covered a mile when they saw Mandalian coming in, and he wasn't walking his horse this time—he was riding like hell.

two

Windy Mandalian's face was taut when he reined in beside Fitzgerald. There was no fright in his weathered eyes, but a deal of electric excitement.

"Found him, Lieutenant."

"Wraps-Up-His-Tail?"

"None other. Four miles south by west. He's got his camp in a wash near to Three Knolls. Don't think we would have found him if it wasn't for the tracks that Sioux left. You come up on it real sudden—I was damn near in their camp before I saw it."

"Where's Hatchet?"

"He's holding things down, sir. I left him in a thicket and give him word to ride like hell if they came up out of that wash. I don't 'spect they will, though. I'm almost sure they didn't see us."

"Four miles off, did you say?" Fitzgerald looked to the darkening skies.

"That's right, sir. More or less. Night will likely be on us before we draw up to the wash."

"Yes. We'll ride to high ground and make night camp. No smoke, no talking. I want to hit them at first light."

"That's the best way," Windy agreed. The scout wiped his forehead on his buckskin sleeve. Glancing at Fitzgerald, he told him reluctantly, "We've got us a small problem with this, Lieutenant."

"A problem?"

"Yes, sir." Windy studied the detachment. "They outnumber us maybe three to one. He's got more'n a hundred braves in camp. Mixed Sioux, Crow, Cheyenne, and I b'lieve an Arapaho or two."

A hundred braves. That sank in slowly. Windy's informant hadn't believed there were half that many. Possibly more had drifted in while they searched out Wraps-Up-His-Tail, seeking to share in the medicine man's magic.

There would be no women and children in his camp. This was a war camp, with Wraps-Up-His-Tail exhorting his recruits, promising them vengeance, promising them many coups, great magic. When he judged that he had enough recruits, the Crow would lead them on a reign of terror, until a lucky bullet proved his magic false. Of course, by then it would be too late for those who had died before his guns.

"What's the nearest settlement, Windy?"

"White settlement? Carson Springs, I reckon." Windy scratched his neck. "You want to send word over there?"

"No. Let's just make sure Wraps-Up-His-Tail never gets there. I want the man, Windy. I want him bad. When we go in, come morning, I want that man. I don't give a damn if every other brave gets out of that camp alive. But Wraps-Up-His-Tail has got to leak some magic."

"All right," Windy agreed. The lieutenant was right, he knew. This band of hostiles, a mixed contingent of renegades, would likely disperse once their leader was dead. Wraps-Up-His-Tail was the primary target, the horses were secondary. Cavalry has a hell of a time fighting without horses, and they would be a priority target, as they always were.

Night camp was a half-mile away from the wash, downwind so that the dogs and horses in the Indian war camp could not catch their scent on the night breeze. By the last light of day, Windy sketched out a plan of the camp for

Lieutenant Fitzgerald, showing him the location of the largest tent, which presumably belonged to Wraps-Up-His-Tail, and the location of the horses.

"If we take the medicine man down, and manage to get those horses out of the camp, there's every chance of bringing them in without much shooting," Fitzgerald believed.

Windy wasn't so optimistic, but he agreed there was a chance. "Only if we get Wraps-Up-His-Tail, I think, Lieutenant. If we can come up on them without being spotted, they might throw down their guns, figuring to live to fight another day."

"With a little luck."

"Yes, sir. Always with a little luck."

Fitzgerald was a good officer, no matter what a grumbler like Dillson thought. He didn't want to go down in a blaze of glory. The greatest glory was in handling this with the fewest casualties possible. It was never painless to watch the dirt shoveled onto a man in a blue uniform. Fitzgerald had seen enough of that to last him a lifetime. Yet he was not dreamer enough to hope that tomorrow would bring no casualties. He unrolled his bed and stretched out, not sleeping, but watching the cold, high stars for a long while.

Private Dillson wasn't sleeping, either. His anger, far from burning out, was constantly fed with slights real or imagined from Dillson's memory. He wondered, with dark anticipation, what would happen in the morning.

It could be that Lieutenant Fitzgerald would be shot in action. He doubted that anyone could ever prove it was an army weapon that took him down. Even if they did, it had happened plenty of times in the past—an officer hit by friendly fire. Hell, that was how Stonewall Jackson got his.

Dillson smiled at the thought, trying to picture how he would react. "Hell, boys, I didn't have much use for the man, but I sure didn't want to see him shot by them hostiles." He chuckled out loud, and Reb McBride, the nearest man to him, hissed:

"Shut up, Dillson. What's so damned funny?"

"Nothin', Texas. Nothin' at all." Then he chuckled again

17

and rolled onto his side, the warmth of his smoldering hatred comforting him in the chill of the dark night.

Despite the excitement, Lieutenant Fitzgerald slept well also. He focused his thoughts on the luxuries awaiting him in Kansas City, and shut out any creeping apprehensions of tomorrow. Maybe, he thought, Matt Kincaid could be induced to switch furloughs. He doubted it, but Fitzgerald dwelled on the fantasy anyway.

Then this expedition could be Fitzgerald's last before furlough. He would talk to Matt. It couldn't hurt. So then, if Captain Conway got back to Number Nine on schedule, and the replacement officer showed up on time...Fitzgerald yawned and fell back into a deep sleep, haunted by soft dreams of satin and silk.

Captain Warner Conway was of a mind to push on into Outpost Number Nine. Darkness was falling rapidly, however, and he knew the women would be tired. He glanced back toward the ambulance where they rode, recalling that on the few occasions he had tried it, he had found himself more exhausted at the end of the day than he would have been sitting a good, easy-gaited horse.

"What do you think, Mr. Haversham? Shall we camp?"

The young second lieutenant was agreeable. "Whatever you prefer, sir. The ladies might wish to step down rather than wait until we reach the outpost."

Conway nodded, hiding a faint smile. The shavetail would as readily have agreed to drive on to Number Nine if Conway had shown an inclination to do so. He was a bright, well-trained young man. A West Pointer did not volunteer his opinion to a senior officer unless it was asked for, and if the senior officer proposed to go right, a bright second lieutenant did not suggest that left would be better.

"I think up ahead, near the river, Private," Conway told the ambulance driver.

"Yes, sir," the soldier responded.

Conway swung his horse slightly northward toward the river crossing, where a stand of oak and a single stunted

18

cedar would provide a windbreak. Haversham followed suit, as did the two privates on horseback. Officially escorts for their party, the two men would simply be detached to Conway's command, rather than be made to take the long ride back to Fort Laramie.

"Lieutenant Kincaid will have to pace the floor another night," Conway told Haversham. The young lieutenant smiled. Warner Conway had spoken so much of Kincaid, Fitzgerald, and Sergeant Cohen since leaving Laramie that Haversham felt as if he knew them well already. Undoubtedly they would not match his mental image of them, but for now those images seemed alive and definitive in his mind.

"He's had a long wait for furlough, as have you all," Haversham commented.

"You'll be a popular man for a time," Conway told him. "A saving angel in blue."

The ambulance driver had drawn up beside the river, which sparkled in the late sunlight, and Warner Conway halted his mount and swung down, walking to the back of the light vehicle.

The door swung open and Flora emerged, travel-weary but smiling. Then Mrs. Haversham stepped out, and despite himself, Warner Conway found his eyes alert, his pulse rising slightly.

She took her husband's hand, squinted into the sunlight streaming through the oaks, and stepped down, a brilliant smile on her lips.

Catha Haversham was a full-blooded Cherokee, no more than twenty years old, with wide dark eyes, full sensuous lips, and a perfect, high-breasted figure. She was utterly beautiful, her complexion smooth, creamy, the shade of milk and tea, with a soft glow underneath her skin, the result of perfect health.

Everett Haversham had been married to her for three short months, and when he helped her down, his eyes were starry, as if he still found her overwhelming.

"There now," Catha said with a smile that charmed both

19

the men and Flora Conway, "and didn't I need a stretch! Are we far from the outpost, Captain Conway?"

"We'll have an hour or two's travel in the morning, Mrs. Haversham," Warner Conway answered. He was aware of Flora's eyes on him as he looked into the unbearably young, beautiful face of Catha.

"You musn't call me Mrs. Haversham, Captain. I've already told your wife. Everyone must call me Catha, please. I want to know you all and have you all as friends. So please, if you must be formal with Everett for military reasons, do so. But let me be Catha to you."

She stuck out a hand and took Captain Conway's briefly, her smile warm, her eyes innocent and compelling. Conway held the hand magnetically for a moment and then dropped it, feeling as flustered as a schoolboy.

If Catha Haversham was aware that she had that effect on men, she didn't show it. She hooked her arm around her husband's elbow and they walked toward the river, speaking quietly. Without realizing it, Warner Conway let his eyes follow her, fascinated at a primitive level by the fluid swaying of her hips.

Flora cleared her throat, and Captain Conway turned his head sharply, encountering her knowing smile.

"She's an interesting woman," Conway said rapidly. "Do you find her interesting?"

"Yes," Flora said, suppressing her smile. "But not nearly so fascinating as you seem to, Warner."

He laughed ineffectively. "I just want her to feel welcome. She's so young. Did you think—? Flora!" He put his arm around his wife's shoulder, and kissed her forehead lightly.

"She is beautiful, Warner."

"Well, if you like that type."

"Are we likely to find a man who *doesn't* like Catha's type?"

Dusk was purpling the plains. The few high clouds were crimson and gold. Doves winged homeward, low against the sky. Warner Conway and Flora walked along the river a little way, while the three privates built the fire and un-harnessed the ambulance horse.

Conway stopped when they had rounded a small bend in the river and could no longer be seen from camp. He put his hands on Flora's shoulders and kissed her. Then he held her tightly, watching the sky, the sunlight twinkling on the slowly flowing river.

"You're the only girl for me, Flora Conway."

"Oh, I know that, Warner. But dear Catha is an extraordinary beauty."

"No more beautiful than you, Flora."

She laughed. "Perhaps I am that beautiful in your dreams, dear Warner." She added, "Or in mine."

"She's young, beautiful, and very much in love with a personable young officer," Conway said. "I don't envy them. I am happy for them. And I remember our first years, I suppose. Living on nothing, waiting for a promotion."

"As we are now," Flora said with humor.

"Yes." He kissed her again. "But we endured. Grew a little older, a little wiser. And by God, we *lived* those years, didn't we, Flora?"

She nodded her agreement, a hundred small remembrances filling her mind. She stretched upward on tiptoes and kissed his ear lightly, and whispered, "I can't wait to get back home to our own bed. I would have ridden all night without complaint."

"Woman, you're insatiable!" He held her at arm's length. "I thought you would have had enough in Denver."

"No, but it was nice, wasn't it?"

"No reveille."

"No Sergeant Cohen tapping at the door in the middle of the night."

"Restaurant cooking."

"But not quite as good as home."

"No. Not quite as good as being home. Even if home is only old Number Nine."

He put his arm around his wife's waist and they walked back toward the camp, through the settling shadows. After leaving her at their fire, he went to make a tour of the camp. The coffee was already boiling over a low, flickering fire. One of the privates, the small man named Duckworth, was pouring himself a cup.

"Not quite ready, sir," Duckworth said, coming erect. "Me, I couldn't wait. It's been a long day on the heels of one just as long."

"It was," Captain Conway agreed. "I don't think I'll wait, either. Pour me one, will you, Private Duckworth?"

"Yes, sir," the kid replied.

As represented, the coffee was thin, but hot, and Conway sipped at it. The night would be cool and clear. As they drew nearer to the outpost, he found himself eager to be there, to be behind his desk—which seemed incredible, considering how anxiously he and Flora had awaited this often-postponed trip.

He was silent, watching the land grow dark. Flora had gone back to the ambulance to collect her toilet articles. He had almost forgotten about Duckworth until the voice at his elbow asked:

"Is it bad out there, sir? As bad as they say?"

"It can be, Duckworth."

Captain Conway glanced at the kid. In the feeble light he looked drawn, and excessively young. "But I'm sure you can handle it. You look like a soldier. Just listen to your sergeant and your platoon leader. You'll cut it."

"Thank you, sir," Duckworth beamed. He seemed to stand a little taller now, and he turned on his heel, walking back to where the other enlisted men sat eating. Conway smiled and strode to his own fire, where Haversham was just now helping Catha to a seat next to Flora, on an ancient, skinned log. The fire dancing on her face completed the illusion. Catha was the timeless, beautiful savage of the romantics. A Cherokee princess. A noble, earthy creature.

Haversham stood transfixed by her beauty, hovering over her devotedly, his eyes enchanted.

"Well, this will be our last meal on the trail for a while," Warner Conway said.

"I can't wait," Catha said. "It's all so exciting. For Everett and me."

"I only hope you're not disappointed," Conway said. "Outpost Number Nine is a little rough. I suppose Flora has told you about your quarters."

"Oh yes," Catha said with genuine enthusiasm. "She cautioned me that I might find them dreary, but then she went on to describe the sod roof, the rough planking. It sounds delightful to me."

Warner Conway shook his head in vague puzzlement, and Catha went on, speaking in a low but lively voice as the fire guttered. "You see, Captain Conway, I never lived in a frame house before I married Everett. I was a reservation Cherokee. If you think Outpost Number Nine might sound a little rough for me, you should see the house I lived in before Everett found me! Ask him, he'll tell you."

"It's true," Everett agreed. "Brush and poles. But out of that house came the most beautiful woman in the world."

"Thank you, Everett. But you see, Captain, Flora, it's true. Outpost Number Nine will be a fine home for me. Four walls, a woodstove, a full pantry. It's all anyone needs, really." She hunched forward slightly, arms crossed beneath her breasts, the fire bright on her animated face. "And that is what I want to get across to my brothers."

Conway looked at her blankly. "You have brothers coming north?"

Catha laughed, and it was a rich, sparkling laugh.

Conway glanced expectantly at Lieutenant Haversham.

"She uses the word in a broader sense, sir," Haversham said.

"Yes," Catha explained. "All Indians are brothers—or sisters, as the case may be. One reason I am so looking forward to coming north is that it gives me the opportunity to speak to the Plains tribes, to explain what the Cherokee have done." She moved her hands in emphatic, chopping motions, her eyes intent. "I want to tell them how the Cherokee have modified their culture, accepted what is good in American civilization—houses, agriculture, the husbandry

23

of animals, instead of the precarious life of nomadic hunters."

"I hardly think—" Conway began, but Catha, her next thought running close behind the last, interrupted him.

"You see, all this needless bloodshed could be avoided. Their way is the old way, and it is going, no matter how they cling to it. The new way is good for everyone, white and Indian."

When her enthusiasm had dwindled enough to allow it, Conway commented, "That would certainly simplify my life, Catha. Much of our problem is based on the collision of cultures. Yet, in all candor, I must tell you that these Plains tribes are a far cry from the Indians you know. There is a tradition of nomadic existence, and of the hunt as a way of life. There is also, I'm afraid, a strong tradition of warfare as sport.

"Before the coming of the horse and the gun, it was sport. The Crow raided the Nez Perce, the Sioux raided the Cheyenne. Horses and women were taken, coups counted. It balanced out in the end, I suppose. Yet now the sport is gone, and only the war continues. It is a tradition that will lead to the demise of the Plains culture. And we at Number Nine, unfortunately, are the cutting edge of the new civilization."

"I don't see where we disagree," Catha said lightly.

"Where we disagree, Catha, is that I believe nothing can be said at this point to bring about a peaceful solution. It is tragic but true. The men we deal with are cunning, proud, but above all else, they are warriors. And quite savage in their warfare."

"All that scalping and mutilation, you mean," Catha said, shaking her head. "I can't believe all those gruesome tales, can you, Everett?"

"Yes," the young officer said thoughtfully. He smiled, his blue eyes clouded with vague concern. "Captain Conway has told me some tales that can curl your hair."

"Even if they are true," Catha said, switching tacks conveniently, "I am sure that if my brothers in Dakota were

24

shown that their way is not the best, they are intelligent enough and frank enough to change. Surely," she said, looking from one unconvinced face to another, "if it were for the good of all the people, for the good of the tribe they are fighting to sustain! To live well, happily, rather than starve and eventually die. I believe you underestimate the common sense of the Indian."

"Men aren't necessarily governed by common sense, Catha," Warner Conway put in. "Them or us. Tradition, blind allegiance to custom and superstition—even simple habit—seem to have more weight in our lives than reason. Or don't you agree?"

"Oh, I quite agree, Captain Conway. And such influences will dominate until logic is presented, a logic counter to habit, a logic that deflates superstition."

Flora Conway spoke for the first time, seeing that the conversation had reached an impasse. "Perhaps all this will be resolved in time—let us hope so. But for now, dear Catha, I think we would do well to rest. Tomorrow comes quickly, no matter what it brings. And," she said, covering a yawn with her fist, "I, for one, am weary. Excuse me."

"Quite right, Flora," Captain Conway said, rising. "I'll walk you to the ambulance."

Haversham and Catha had risen as Conway did. Now they exchanged a secret look and Flora, noticing it, said easily, "I think I would like to sleep out tonight, Warner. It's a lovely evening."

It was getting as cold as hell, but Warner Conway said nothing. He caught the hint in Flora's glance and he nodded. "All right. I'll have your bed rolled out."

Conway had started to turn away, but he halted and said over his shoulder, quite casually, "You may as well sleep in the ambulance with your wife, Haversham."

"Yes, sir," Haversham agreed quickly. He nearly stumbled over the log as he went to his wife, putting an arm around her waist, guiding her back to the ambulance, her head on his shoulder.

"You're a romantic, Flora," Warner Conway said, the

fondness he felt for his wife obvious in his tone.

"Incurably," she agreed. She watched as Catha Haversham, preceding her husband into the enclosed ambulance, lifted a hand. Flora waved back and sighed; feeling her husband's arm around her, she leaned her head back against his chest and sighed. "I'm feeling a bit romantic tonight myself," she said in a soft whisper.

"There's only one ambulance, unfortunately," Conway replied. He glanced around, saw the enlisted men already stretched out in their beds across the oak grove, and gently kissed Flora's neck, sending a chill along her spine.

"There's all outdoors," she whispered, turning to face him.

"With the men... it's damned cold out, Flora," he objected. She kissed him and then drew back, studying his lean, weathered face.

"How age does creep up on us. I can recall the time you would have run off into the woods with me, Warner."

"If you can endure another day, my darling," he said kissing her, "I shall make it up to you, I promise."

She kissed him in return. "If that is a definite promise."

"Most definite."

She smiled, took his arm, and turned toward the flat, grassy clearing where they would make their beds. Flora said nothing as they walked to the clearing.

"Jealous of Catha?" Conway asked teasingly.

"Heavens, no!" she said, meaning it. "I have you, after all, my dear commanding officer." She was silent for a moment; then, from out of the darkness, she said, "But I am a trifle worried about the girl. She has the strangest ideas—well, you heard some of them tonight."

"She's young," Conway answered. "Idealistic. But she's bright, very bright. She'll hold her ideas as long as they conform with reality, I expect, and when she sees enough, understands enough how things really are, she'll quietly drop her ideas. Lord, I can recall all the ways I was going to solve this problem and end the fighting when we first arrived!"

"You're right, of course," Flora said from her bed. She watched the silent stars, listened to the hooting between a pair of courting owls, and pulled her blanket higher. "Still, Warner, I worry. I know she means well..." She realized then that Warner Conway was asleep beside her, breathing deeply, softly. She smiled, liking the familiar, comforting sound of him at rest, then closed her own eyes and rolled over, letting her concerns over Catha Haversham tumble into the dark repository of sleep.

Her breathing was soft, but the tempo of it increased, her eyes shining in the darkness, as Everett, seated on the bunk, unhooked her dress and let it slide to the floor of the ambulance.

She helped him with her shift, their fingers meeting anxiously as they worked toward a common purpose. The chemise followed the dress, rustling to the floor, and Catha stood there before him, naked and proud, her smooth, flat abdomen accepting his kisses. His hands rested on her hips, and when he glanced up, she was looking down at him with the faintest of smiles. Her straight white teeth showed through a gap between her full lips. Her eyes were dark, glowing with sensuality. Her hair, undone, flowed down over her shoulders and across her breasts in a rich, glossy cascade.

Catha bent to him, and her breasts brushed his lips. He rose to them eagerly, running admiring hands along their firm, full contours, his lips finding her taut, dark nipples as his heart hammered.

"Am I still beautiful?" she asked, her voice a purr as her fingers toyed with his curly blond hair.

"Perfect. Perfectly beautiful, Catha. I can hardly keep my hands off you day or night, no matter the place."

"And now it is night," she said with a soft, murky laugh. "Now we are alone in our shelter."

His hands fell from her breasts and dove between her legs, exploring the luxuriant, dark bush there before finding the honey-sweet inner recesses of her body.

27

He touched her there for a while, his head against her soft abdomen. Catha lifted herself slightly, spreading her thighs as he probed deeply, running searching fingers along her silky, warm flesh. The blood raced in his temples, throbbed in his groin, as his erection fought against the restraining fabric of his trousers.

He fell back, drawing Catha to him, and as he settled on the cot, he felt her fingers, light as butterflies, reach for his fly and unbutton it to release the straining flesh.

She straddled him, reaching behind her to pull down his trousers, which he kicked off, unbuttoning his shirt as her lips followed each button down his chest, nuzzling the blond hair that curled there.

He reached up, finding her neck and face through the dark veil of her hair, and drew her mouth to his, kissing her hungrily, greedily, wanting to devour her, to possess her beauty, her womanliness completely.

Her lips were soft, supple, magic, and he felt an insistent throbbing in his loins. Reaching down, he found her crotch and spread her, wondering at the softness, the warm readiness of her.

"Can't you wait, darling?" she whispered into his ear, pausing to bite the lobe, to let her tongue follow the whorl of his ear.

"No," he said, his voice constricted, his breathing ragged. "Can you?"

"No." She breathed the word into his mouth and followed the whisper with a searching, fluid kiss. He felt Catha's hand run across his abdomen, his thigh, to join his own hand.

He felt her raise her hips, and then felt her nimble fingers on his erection, lifting him, positioning him, and he held his breath.

The head of his member met the tantalizing heat of Catha's body, and he shuddered as she settled onto him, enveloping him with her warmth, the spell of her magic.

She sat up, and he could see the smile on her lips, the distant, haunted light in her eyes. By the faint glow the silver moon cast through the high window of the ambulance, he could see her bite at her lip as, rapt in concentration, she slowly lifted her hips and then, just as slowly, settled once again onto his shaft.

Her palms rested on his abdomen; his own hands touched her where they came together, feeling the growing dampness. He felt the surging in his loins rising, the spasmodic need to consummate the act pulse within him, but he held back, his eyes watching with utter fascination as Catha, his Catha, his beautiful Catha, swayed and thrust against him, her eyes, unfocused it seemed, deep in the luxury of sensuality, her breasts swaying slightly, a low murmur growing in her throat as she found the rhythm, the bundle of nerve endings she wanted.

The night was cool, but where her hips spread across his pelvis, a focus of intense heat demanded more of him, and he arched his back, driving deeply into her, feeling her hands against his chest, her thighs against his, the answering rhythm of her hips, until he could no longer hold back if his life depended on it.

She felt him reaching the point of no return, and she encouraged him. "Now. That's my baby. More. Let it all go," and she made a small sound of gratitude or sheer joy deep in her throat—a sort of humming, musical sound that broke off into a cry of passion as he came and she fell shuddering against him.

They lay together, their breathing rapid, ragged, their bodies cooling in the night. His hand held her head close to his throat, and he felt her breath mist against him, felt the soft veil of her dark hair spread out across his chest, and Everett Haversham felt very pleased with himself, his wife, his life, and all of creation.

three ———————————————

McBride felt a hand on his shoulder, and he struggled out of the vivid, confused dream of his dusty, hardscrabble Texas home. He rubbed his eyes and sat upright in the dark chill of morning.

"Mount up," Gus Olsen said, and Reb nodded, stretching the sleep from his night-chilled muscles. When he could feel his blood begin to circulate, he rolled his bed up and staggered toward his horse, moving silently among other sleep-drugged men.

A silver half moon was sinking into the oaks to the west. A low ground fog twisted along the bottoms, ghostly, pale and cold.

"It'll warm up soon enough," Rafferty said, as if reading his thoughts. Rafferty looked terrible by the pale moonlight. His face was drawn, his dark eyes circled with shadow.

The trembling that was in Reb McBride from the cold night gave way to another sort of trembling. The realization that battle, bloodshed—possibly his own death—came with the dawn, filled his body briefly with involuntary spasms. The animal organism revolting against a mind that would drag it forward into pain and death.

Reb smoothed his saddle blanket and saddled up, kneeing

his bay in the belly to force the extra air out of the balky horse, who had learned this maneuver to avoid the tight bite of the cinch.

Fitzgerald had been up first, apparently. He was mounted, shaven; stiff in the saddle, he rode among the troopers, eyes searching, an occasional whispered encouragement drifting across the clearing.

Reb McBride noticed the other man as well. His eyes, which seemed murderous, were fixed magnetically on Lieutenant Fitzgerald, and Reb felt a wave of trepidation as he watched Dillson. Was the man capable of...? Reb knew he was. Frowning deeply, he swung into the saddle, forming up beside Rafferty and Dobbs.

There was no speaking. With hand signs, Fitzgerald and then Gus Olsen moved them out, with only the clinking of the lieutenant's saber, the creaking of saddle leather to crease the silence.

They passed out through the oaks and dipped down into the shallow wash beyond. There, the ground fog moved among them, spinning apprehension, chilling them with cold, searching fingers.

Fitzgerald was at the head of the column, Windy Mandalian and Gus Olsen flanking him. Their horses were lost in the wraiths of fog, only their heads and shoulders visible. The coulee, where Wraps-Up-His-Tail's camp still slept, lay a quarter of a mile off. The land, spotted with cheat grass, stunted sage, and catclaw, rose gradually. The broken limbs of a dead cottonwood stood out against the dark skies.

Fitzgerald felt the dampness penetrate his tunic and trickle coldly down his chest and back. His horse was impatient, sidestepping anxiously, and Fitzgerald patted the big bay's neck.

Suddenly a painted face appeared out of the fog like a summoned demon. Fitzgerald blinked and then grabbed for his Schofield, for already the Indian had heeled his pony away, and was riding flat out for the coulee.

"Dammit!" Fitzgerald cursed. Windy Mandalian had his rifle to his shoulder, but Fitzgerald put his hand on the barrel of the scout's Sharps. "The shot will warn them sooner than he can."

Reb McBride heard a muffled curse from the front of the column and, looking up, saw Windy raise his rifle. He didn't fire, but as Reb watched, the scout pumped his rifle over his head, alerting everyone that hostiles had been sighted. Reb's Springfield rifle was cool in his hand, and he held to it tightly as Fitzgerald lifted the platoon into a canter.

They rode across the cold earth, their hoofs like muffled thunder. McBride saw the coulee suddenly appear before them and, at the same moment, became aware of three mounted Indians riding hard away from them, to the south. They were still naked from sleeping, but they hadn't forgotten their rifles.

Shots winged back and forth between the soldiers and the fleeing Indians, and Fitzgerald sent four men after them.

Looking around, the lieutenant spotted McBride and Dillson. "Get down the wash! I want that medicine man!"

McBride spurred his horse down the wash, not looking to see if Dillson was on his heels. He angled north and toward the big tent. In the camp, all was confusion. Men vaulted to their horses and spun in circles.

Fitzgerald's main party appeared on the rim, and the Indians, firing on the run, made for the cottonwoods beyond the camp or tried the coulee to the south. But Fitzgerald had already pinched off that escape route, and the Indians trying that met fierce resistance.

Fitzgerald led the charge down the sandy bluff, anger riding him, anger that this had not been accomplished bloodlessly. He saw Private McCormack, behind him and to his right, being dragged by his horse, saw another soldier pitch face-forward down the bluff to be trampled by those behind him.

In the Indian camp, rifles barked, and he knew they were repeaters, and again he cursed the stumbling bureaucracy that issued Spencers to the agency Indians and left his own men armed with the converted Springfield single-shots.

32

Fitzgerald charged on, wanting to get near enough so that his men could unlimber their pistols, cutting the Indians' advantage.

He had lost his hat somewhere and now, turning in the saddle, hair in his eyes, he searched for Wraps-Up-His-Tail, knowing that the death of the medicine man could bring this to an end.

The camp was a swirl of bloody confusion. Stretch Dobbs rode through a tipi, exchanging fire with a brave hidden there, and Fitzgerald saw Gus Olsen slapped back by a bullet, which flooded his shirt with instant crimson blood.

Fitzgerald himself banged away with his Schofield, catching a running brave as he darted for the cottonwoods, sending the warrior sprawling, his arm blown half away.

Windy Mandalian, riding low on his appaloosa's neck, pursued his man—a rangy, naked Sioux—into the cotton-woods.

The Sioux leaped a low limb, crashed into the under-brush, and fired back wildly over his shoulder, the bullet singing past Windy's ear.

Windy bucked his horse into the brush and instantly knew he had made a mistake. He had passed under a cottonwood, and from the corner of his eye he saw the blur of copper flesh and scarlet paint, and the brave hit him, slamming the scout from his horse.

Windy rolled to his feet as his horse, kicking up its heels, danced away into the brush. The Sioux was standing facing him, his rifle at waist level.

Windy's Sharps lay in the sand fifteen feet away, but an instant reflex, bred in a hundred Indian battles, saved him. The warrior touched off a shot so close that it tugged at Windy's buckskin jacket, but the scout's hand had drawn his murderously sharp bowie from its sheath, and he had already, without thinking consciously, calculated the distance between himself and the brave. He judged it to be a turn and a half, and with a flick of his wrist he threw the knife.

The rifle in the brave's hands exploded again, the bullet

33

whining off the tree at Windy's back as the bowie drove deeply into the Sioux's chest, severing the aorta.

The Sioux tumbled back, dead before he hit the sandy earth, his heart futilely pumping blood as Windy, striding to him, withdrew the knife with some difficulty.

He plunged the knife into the sand to clean it, then recovered his rifle and returned to the saddle.

The fight in the coulee sounded like the Fourth of July from the far bluff where McBride and Dillson worked through the brush and trees. They could see the frantic activity, see men lying on the ground, but it was too far away to have the impact of reality.

Far up the coulee, there was sporadic firing at the point where the Indians had tried to break out, but that was already dying down.

Dillson had dismounted, and now Reb followed suit. They ground-tethered their horses and took up a position on an outcropping of granite. From there they overlooked the entire battle, and could see all the trails leading out of the valley.

"See him?"

"Uh-uh. Nothing."

Their eyes swept the low brush. The Crow medicine man was either dead in the camp or, for some inexplicable reason, had been absent from it when Fitzgerald attacked.

"He could've gotten out," Dillson whispered.

"Don't see how," Reb countered.

They sat on the rock, the gnats bothering them, the rising sun warm. They were isolated from the battle, and it was eerie to watch men fall, claw at each other hand to hand, and die.

McBride got to his belly and swiveled slightly northward. There was a game trail winding through head-high willow brush, and he tried to follow it with his eyes, guessing at its direction by measuring the terrain. Nothing. He lost the trail, but was certain by the silence that no one was on it.

The brush was thick, and anything above the size of a rabbit would sound like a grizzly coming that way. He could only conclude that Wraps-Up-His-Tail was lying low, yet that seemed senseless. Fitzgerald would certainly detail a search party.

McBride swiveled back and his breath caught.

He froze, his eyes wide, his heart pounding. Dillson had his rifle to his shoulder, and was sighting down the long blue barrel. Fitzgerald!

Lieutenant Fitzgerald was riding along the trail below and to the south of them, and Dillson was following him with the bead of his front sight.

McBride was temporarily stunned into immobility, but now he coiled his muscles, ready to leap forward and slap the rifle out of Dillson's hands. The big man's bulldog face was molded into a grin of savage glee. His black eyes were absolutely feral.

McBride started his move. He crawled forward, his hand stretching out toward the Springfield in Dillson's hands. Simultaneously he was aware of Fitzgerald, drawing nearer to them, his head turned in the opposite direction.

Reb reached out, yanked hard on Dillson's shoulder, and caught an elbow to the face for his trouble. Reb's own rifle clattered away down the rock, and Fitzgerald's head came around at the sound.

In horror, Reb watched as Dillson, squinting into the sun, pulled the trigger. The muzzle flash was so near to Reb's face that it singed him. The report thundered in his ears and McBride saw Dillson, obscured by a cloud of black-powder smoke, get to his feet.

Clawing toward Dillson, Reb turned his eyes to Fitzgerald. He blinked, shook his head, and blinked again. Fitzgerald was still astride his horse, and now he waved a hand at them.

It was only then that Reb McBride saw the other figure. He lay twisted in the brush beside the trail. A splash of yellow ocher paint decorated his copper face.

It was Wraps-Up-His-Tail, and his magic had failed him. Dillson shoveled a fresh cartridge into his Springfield and turned to Reb, his face dark and expressionless.

"You damned near ruined that, McBride."

"I'm sorry." Reb stood, letting the wind wash over him. He looked again at Fitzgerald, who was loading the Crow medicine man onto his shying horse, then back at Dillson, who was calmly rolling a smoke. "I'm sorry, Dillson. Hell, I thought . . ."

And then, looking at Dillson's face, Reb was less than certain that he had made a mistake at all. The big man's expression was of mingled pleasure and sardonic disgust. With Fitzgerald? With himself? Reb could not be sure.

"I know what you thought." Dillson caught up the reins to his horse and hooked his rifle onto the spider. Below, the battle was rapidly dying. Fitzgerald had ridden into the center of the camp and flung the dead medicine man to the ground. The sight of him had caused a good many of the remaining Indians to throw their weapons down and surrender.

"You know?" Reb said. He stepped into leather and eyed the big man.

"Sure." Dillson threw his smoke away and turned his horse. "You thought I was going to kill the lieutenant."

"Yes. I never saw Wraps-Up-His-Tail." They rode silently down through the brush. Crossing a dry streambed, Reb finally got up the courage to ask, "Were you going to kill him?"

Dillson looked offended. "Nah," he said. "Kill Fitzgerald? Nah . . . not with no witness around."

Then he rode ahead, whistling a dry little tune, and McBride watched him, feeling his skin crawl.

The captured Indians sat crosslegged in the clearing, guards posted around them. A burial detail was digging graves in the sand for the Indians. The two dead soldiers would be transported back to Outpost Number Nine.

Gus Olsen looked like hell. He sat against the trunk of a wind-ruffled cottonwood, his sleeve cut away, blood stain-

36

ing the white bandage. "Damn, damn, damn," Olsen repeated, his teeth clenched against the pain.

"Break it?" Reb asked, nodding at the arm.

"Looks like. Tore it up real good anyway," Jefferson answered.

They heard the sound of approaching horses now, and looked to the south, watching the incoming patrol. A dozen surly Sioux and Arapaho rode with them. Fitzgerald walked over to meet the party, which was led by Rafferty and Corporal Miller.

Miller reported without swinging down. "No casualties, sir." Fitzgerald's face sagged with relief. "I estimate a dozen hostiles escaped before we could pinch off the coulee. There's three dead Indians up there."

"Very good, Corporal," Fitzgerald answered. "Dismount your prisoners and put them with the others. Shoot their ponies. We'll give them a good long walk back to Number Nine. They can think about what they've done on the way."

The burial detail, sleeves rolled up, came to pick up Wraps-Up-His-Tail. They had a sheet of canvas stretched out, and they bent to roll him onto it.

"Not him," Fitzgerald said harshly. They glanced up at him in surprise. The dark eyes of the hostiles were on the officer as well. "Leave him to them." He lifted his chin to the sky, where a dozen black vultures circled patiently.

The burial detail went on to the next man, and Fitzgerald turned, confronting the renegades. "He deserves no burial, no ceremony, no dignity. Wraps-Up-His-Tail led his people and yours to death with his lies."

Then Fitzgerald turned and stalked away, waiting in the shade while the burial detail finished up. The Indians were herded together and their ponies were led off. After a time they heard the fusillade of shots, the brief, pained complaint of a horse.

They were up onto the flats by noon, leading twenty-two captive renegades, carrying two dead of their own. No one spoke. The dust rose behind them, drifting through the long grass before it settled, leaving no trace of their passing.

37

Fitzgerald turned toward the north, noticing the bulked thunderheads, black against a pale sky. It would rain, and the rain would wash away all signs of the battle. All the little scars man inflicts on the earth are erased in time by soft winds, gentle rain, Fitzgerald thought, until there is nothing left but the bloody memories.

By midafternoon they were in sight of Outpost Number Nine. Home. Fitzgerald smiled at that—Number Nine, a rough final outpost on the Wyoming Plains, home. Well, it was home for now, and it was a welcome sight. Dutch Rothausen would have coffee on, and maybe doughnuts. Tonight they would sleep beneath a roof, have a cot beneath them.

Fitzgerald noticed, without endowing it with any significance, that a half-dozen new tipis had been added to the Indian settlement out beyond the deadline. Probably Cheyenne, spooked by Wraps-Up-His-Tail's war plans. For an Indian who did not want to make war, there was no safer place.

Wraps-Up-His-Tail's war was over, his medicine buried or devoured by buzzards. They were still too far off to be certain, but Fitzgerald had the sudden, warm feeling that the captain was back. He couldn't put his finger on what triggered that belief until they had drawn a half-mile nearer, and then he saw what his subconscious mind had already registered. The ambulance rested just inside the gate; Fitzgerald led his party in, his spirits rising now with each stride of the horse beneath him.

four

Ben Cohen was standing in the orderly room door when Fitzgerald, trail-dusty and weary, swung down. Before he had hit the ground, Lieutenant Fitzgerald called to the first soldier, "Sergeant Olsen's hit, see if your missus can tend him."

Cohen saluted and turned toward his quarters. Fitzgerald had told him by his manner of speaking that Olsen's wound wasn't critical. If it had been, Fitzgerald would have called for Sergeant Rothausen, the cook. In lieu of a surgeon, such tasks fell to Rothausen. Not that he had anything approaching a bedside manner, but he had had a deal of experience butchering, and that bone-saw of Rothausen's had taken off more limbs than any surgeon west of the Mississippi.

"Maggie!" Ben Cohen swung open the door to his quarters. His wife turned to him, her blue Irish eyes sparkling but clouded, sensing the urgency in Ben's voice.

"What is it?"

"Gus Olsen. Gather up your needle and flour, better grab some fresh bandages as well."

He had noticed immediately that Maggie had her new green silk dress on, the one that had come all the way from St. Louis.

She turned her back to her husband. "Unbutton me, Ben.

I was going to visit the new young lieutenant and his missus. And I haven't had a moment to talk to Flora . . . ." Her dress was undone and she slipped out of it, Ben's admiring eyes following her as she walked to the closet and pulled out her old calico dress. .

She caught his eyes on her and, surprisingly, blushed. "At a time like this—what kind of man have I married!" she scolded.

"All man and you know it, Maggie Cohen," Ben responded with a gruffness he didn't mean. She was a good woman, straight, reliable, and giving. Beautiful too, he reflected, in a robust way. She exuded health and honest love. There were moments, too many of them, when he didn't pause to remember that—to remember just how lucky he had been to catch Maggie.

She bustled around the room finding the bandages and the flour—which would be used to aid the clotting if necessary—silk thread and a needle.

"Well," she said, turning to him, "you've got work to do too, haven't you?"

He smiled, shook his head, and followed her out the door. She had the bandages in her arms. Her back was straight, her manner purposeful. That, Ben Cohen remarked to himself, is one useful woman.

He swung back into the orderly room, knowing there was no point in following. They would tell him how Gus had fared; he could do nothing Maggie couldn't do better.

He had walked to Matt Kincaid's office—Captain Conway's office when he was working—but, hearing boot heels on the walk, he paused and turned to see Fitzgerald, wearing a new tunic, enter the orderly room.

"The captain in, Sergeant?"

"Lieutenant Kincaid's still holding it down, sir," Cohen advised him. "I don't look for the captain until morning."

"Very well."

Out of habit, Fitzgerald started to rap on the doorframe. Remembering that Warner Conway was not in, he stepped into the commander's office and found Matt Kincaid stand-

40

ing with his hands behind his back, rocking on his heels, staring at the map on the far wall.

"You find Denver on that map?" Fitzgerald asked.

"I'll find it," Matt said, turning, a smile on his tanned face. "And damned soon. Captain's back."

"I heard." Fitzgerald sagged into a chair with a deep sigh.

"You had some trouble," Matt Kincaid said, walking to the captain's leather chair. He reached into the bottom drawer and removed Conway's whiskey bottle. "I don't think the captain would mind if we had a glass, do you?"

"Why don't you ask the captain and find out?" the voice from the doorway asked. Kincaid's head swiveled around and he came to his feet, as did Fitzgerald. Smiling, Warner Conway crossed the room and shook their hands.

"Can't stay out of the saddle, sir?"

"I guess not," Captain Conway answered. He waved Kincaid back into his seat and perched on the table. "I understand we had a big medicine man stirring things up."

"Had, sir," Fitzgerald answered, nodding his thanks for the glass of whiskey Conway poured and handed him. "Until this morning."

"Care to give me the full report?"

Fitzgerald described the battle, the death of Wraps-Up-His-Tail, and added, "I think Private Dillson saved my skin when he shot the medicine man."

"Maybe he's going to get into the swing of things," Kincaid commented dourly.

"Is the man a troublemaker?" Captain Conway asked, catching the undercurrent of disgust in Matt's voice.

"He hasn't . . . adjusted as well as possible. He wants to return to artillery, the way I understand it."

"And the problem is?"

"They don't want him back."

Warner Conway took a deep, slow breath and sipped his whiskey. "I don't want malcontents on this post. Teach him or ship him. Have Ben work on it."

"Yes, sir."

"How many casualties, Lieutenant?"

"Two dead. Three wounded, including Sergeant Olsen. Maggie Cohen's stitching him up now."

"Have Wojensky take over as acting platoon sergeant."

"Yes, sir."

"These hostiles who escaped, Fitz—think they're a menace to us?"

"My guess would be that they'll filter out of the area, sir. Windy concurs in that estimate, figuring that with Wraps-Up-His-Tail's medicine gone, they'll realize they can't fight and win. But," Fitzgerald added with an openhanded gesture, "we know they're renegades, likely run off from their own tribes. They came to fight, sir, and they're liable to carry their intentions through, medicine or no. We'll have to wait and see, I would guess."

"You don't think we can run them down?" Conway asked.

"No, sir. They'll likely split into small parties. Arapaho with Arapaho, Sioux with Sioux, preferring their own kind now that they have no reason left to council."

"You're probably right," Conway agreed. "Unfortunately. I think it would be wise to keep patrols in the field— with no idea of pursuit, though, unless of course that presents itself. But with the purpose of visibility. Perhaps that will discourage these renegades. Matt probably has little interest in any of this right now," Captain Conway said with a wry smile.

Matt turned his eyes to the captain and said with a faint smile, "I have a strong interest in it, sir. I am determined to keep it in the forefront of my mind all the way to Denver and all the way home."

"And while in Denver?" Fitzgerald chided.

"Ah—well, a man can't be a fanatic, Fitz."

"And how *was* Denver, sir?" he asked Conway. "We haven't had a chance for polite conversation."

"Denver was fine. Bustling, wide open, sprawling. A little too much excitement for a married man like myself. For a young buck like you, Matt, I would judge, it is just the spot."

There was a rap on the doorframe and Conway's head came around. "Enter."

Everett Haversham stepped into the room, and Matt and Fitzgerald looked the young shavetail over. Of slight build, he stood with West Point rigidity. He had curly blond hair, closely cropped, and a shadow of pale mustache.

"Forgive me for intruding, if I am, sir," Haversham said. "I knew a patrol had come in, that there had been some action. Since I am to be a part of the operation here, I have taken the liberty of appearing at the debriefing."

"Fine, Haversham. Matt, Fitz, this is Mr. Haversham, the summer relief officer. The man who makes it possible for you to leave, Matt. I'm sure you'll want to welcome him warmly."

"Kincaid," Matt said, rising. They shook hands all around and briefly recapitulated the action of that morning. Haversham listened attentively, interrupting only infrequently to ask incisive questions. Conway decided he liked the young man's manner, his eagerness to learn.

"I appreciate your going over this again, sir," Haversham said. "It is all new to me, and I have much to learn. Down in the Nation we had an entirely different set of problems. An occasional reservation-jumper, but chiefly our problems were with the whites—crooked Indian agents, bad or sometimes stolen beef being sold to our charges, whiskey runners, gun runners. A few ranchers encroaching on reservation land. But hostilities in this larger sense, no."

He shook his head. "As must be obvious, I graduated the Point too late to enter the War, and whatever battle experience I accrue here will be my first action." He was serious when he added, "I mean to do my best. I trust you to advise me."

"You will be so advised," Conway said without a smile. "But we don't intend to send you out on your own, rest assured. You'll take your turn as officer of the day, and if it is necessary to go out, Lieutenant Fitzgerald will be senior officer."

"I won't let anything happen to you, Haversham," Fitzgerald said. "Hell, that'd screw up my furlough." The joke fell flat. Haversham looked at Fitzgerald with genuine perplexity.

Conway started to add something more diplomatic when he suddenly became aware of a shadowy movement near the open door.

He stood and said, "Please come in, Mrs. Haversham."

Catha smiled hesitantly. "I don't want to interrupt, Captain Conway. I suppose I shouldn't have come here. I assumed that Everett and you had not assumed your official duties yet. I'm quite new to the army," she added.

"It's quite all right, Catha. Do come in. Your husband and I have revealed something of ourselves, I suspect. Neither of us could resist the lure of duty. But we are nearly through with our conference."

Conway turned to Fitzgerald and Matt. "Gentlemen, this is Catha Haversham, Mr. Haversham's lovely wife."

Captain Conway hardly needed to tell them she was lovely. Matt had the presence of mind to step forward and present himself, but Fitzgerald seemed entirely undone. He gawked like a sixteen-year-old farm boy. Haversham watched the two of them with pride and not jealousy. He enjoyed presenting Catha to people, to men especially. Their reactions were quite predictable by now. Perhaps if he felt less than sure of her, he wouldn't have enjoyed these moments of introduction, but he knew Catha well enough to know that she was a one-man woman, and that the smiles she flashed so brilliantly upon the others were merely sincere friendliness.

She had other smiles, soft and sultry, which she reserved for her husband alone.

Conway reminded them all, "Flora expects all of you for dinner this evening. Unless, Matt, you cannot suppress your rush toward freedom long enough to await the morning stage."

"That is less difficult, I assure you," Matt said, "now that I've met Mrs. Haversham." He looked directly at Everett as he spoke his compliment, making sure that the second lieutenant knew it was only that and nothing more.

Haversham, Fitzgerald couldn't help but notice, was positively beaming. Lord, either the man had confidence or was a fool. What a woman! Fitz had to fight for his self-control, and he found himself envious of Matt's suave manner, the captain's dignity.

He sighed inaudibly and told himself that Kansas City was less than a month away. He understood there was a woman or two there as well.

Haversham and Catha went out together, and Matt followed, needling Fitzgerald about the packing he had to attend to. Fitzgerald remained with Captain Conway a minute, catching up on the mail that had accumulated, which the lieutenant had not seen either.

Their heads came up jointly at the smart rap on the doorframe. Sergeant Cohen stood there with coffee in his hands.

"Captain, Lieutenant? Thought this might go well."

"Just the ticket, thank you, Sergeant."

Cohen handed Fitzgerald his cup and placed the captain's on his desk, near his elbow. Conway glanced up, surprised to find Cohen still there.

"Was there something else, Sergeant?"

"Yes, sir. Two civilians wanting to see you."

"Civilians? I didn't hear the stage come in."

"They rode in on horseback, sir."

"Very well." Conway put his stack of papers aside and sighed. "Show them in, Sergeant Cohen."

"Yes, sir."

They heard muffled voices in the orderly room and then footsteps approaching. Captain Conway was ready for just about anything or anyone but the two who appeared at his door.

"Captain Warner Conway?" the man asked.

Conway stood, trying to keep the mingled amusement and astonishment from his face. "I am, sir," he replied.

"Ah," the man replied, as if that were secretly significant. He was over sixty, with iron-gray, quite thin hair, probing blue-green eyes, and a narrow face dominated by a hooked nose. He wore an ancient herringbone jacket, hip boots, and a red flannel shirt.

"This is Lieutenant Fitzgerald," Conway said, trying not to stare at the second visitor, who was even more astonishing.

It was a woman of indeterminate age, narrow as a rail, a head shorter than the man beside her. She wore heavy brogans, and a heavy, colorless coat that reached nearly to her knees, as formless as a hanging drape. Below that a brown, shabby skirt hung limply. Pale gray eyes decorated her plain face, peering out at the world through thick bifocals in a wire frame. Her hair, escaping from beneath a man's weathered flop hat, was straight, unevenly cut, and mouse-brown.

Warner Conway took them instantly for would-be homesteaders, uprooted dirt farmers from the heart of Kansas, but he was entirely wrong.

"I am Dr. Karl Schotte," the old man said, extending a weather-browned hand, which Conway took. Schotte gave him a single lifeless pump of the arm, then turned and shook hands with Fitzgerald in the same automatic way. "My assistant, Miss Marlowe."

"Clara Marlowe," she interjected for no obvious reason. Her eyes held a faint accusation, as if she dared Conway to deny her name. Perhaps it was some sort of defense mechanism gone bizarre. Her eyes met his once, sharply, then retreated to a shy distance, as if she were mentally folding her hands and bowing her head.

"Please," Conway offered, "sit down, sir. Tell me what it is I can do for you."

"Thank you very much." Schotte put aside a large leather bag he carried across his shoulder and sat near the captain. Clara remained standing, as if flight might become necessary at any moment.

Schotte fumbled in his bag and produced a letter. "My credentials, sir," he said handing the letter across the desk, "and a note from my superior in the department."

"The department?"

46

"The Interior Department, of course," Schotte said, holding his head imperiously. He hummed to himself and drummed with his fingers on Conway's desk as the captain read the documents.

Fitzgerald was watching his commander's face curiously, and he saw, as the others must have, Captain Conway's face break briefly into broad amusement, then resume its carefully neutral expression.

"Mr. Schotte—" Warner Conway said, putting the paper down.

"Dr. Schotte, if you please," the man corrected him.

"Yes, Dr. Schotte. It says here that you have come to Outpost Nine—" He glanced at the paper again, not believing his own eyes.

"To count the humpies," Schotte said, leaning back, crossing his arms and legs simultaneously.

"I beg your pardon?"

"Humpies. Humpies! Good God, man. To count the humpies."

"Buffalo," Clara put in.

"To count . . . buffalo." Warner Conway glanced at Fitzgerald, who only shrugged, amusement dancing in his eyes.

"Yes, sir. For the Department of the Interior. Miss Marlowe and I have been working our way west for eighteen months, Captain, counting humpies, as I refer to them. Bison. They have humped backs, you see," he explained, his hand hovering over his own narrow back as if speaking to a man who had never seen or imagined a buffalo.

"They are a natural resource of some significance," Clara Marlowe said. Conway glanced at her. She had his interest, and it seemed she would continue, but she stopped with that.

"The buffalo is extremely nomadic, sir," Warner Conway advised them. "It would seem that a herd counted here might very well be the same as one counted twenty miles south. With you on the move and the buffalo on the move, I hardly see—"

"Sir," Schotte interrupted stiffly, "you need hardly tell

47

my associate and me about humpies. They are our business. I do not pretend to tell you yours—whatever that is." He waved a hand carelessly. "I assure you, I have my methods. If my papers are in order," he said, stretching out a hand to receive them from Conway, "I should appreciate being shown to our quarters and I would like to proceed in the morning, with your assistance."

"My assistance?"

Schotte sighed heavily. Clara was nervously cleaning her glasses; without them, her eyes appeared pale and sightless.

"Yes, my dear Captain. Did you not read the letter from the Secretary? Paragraph four—I shall require the aid of two of your men. As beaters, you might say."

"As beaters. To drive the buffalo toward you?"

"Yes, of course," he said wearily. "And to aid in the counting. So then—" He rose abruptly. "I shall expect the men in the morning. Our quarters?" he inquired.

"May I see the letter again?" Captain Conway asked.

Impatiently the man dug the letter out once again and slowly, carefully this time, Warner Conway went over it. "I seem to have no choice."

"Of course not," Schotte answered grandly. "But then, who in his right mind would wish to stand in the way of this noble project?"

"Who indeed. Sergeant Cohen!"

Cohen's face appeared immediately in the doorway. "Yes, sir."

"Find quarters for Dr. Schotte and Miss Marlowe here. They'll be staying for a time."

"Yes, sir."

"And I'll need two men temporarily assigned to help the doctor. Any suggestions?"

"Private Malone is still under barracks confinement, sir."

"What was that for, Sergeant?"

"The whiskey runner, sir," Ben reminded him.

"Good God, still?"

"You gave him six weeks, sir."

"Well, let's give him a small reprieve." Conway had

48

forgotten about that. It never was clear whether Malone had started the trouble or not, but there was a whiskey trader out there somewhere whose jaw was still mending, and Conway hadn't been able to overlook that.

"I won't have a dangerous man working for me," Dr. Schotte said firmly.

"Private Malone is not dangerous, sir," Conway assured him. "Not when he's sober," he added under his breath. Then he asked Ben Cohen, "Who else?"

"Well, there's Holzer, sir. He's mended from that broken ankle, but not enough to ride. Thing is, I didn't think he'd be the right man for the job."

"Why not, if I may inquire?" Schotte asked.

"Wolfgang Holzer speaks very little English, Doctor. He was recruited off the docks the minute he set foot in America. He had no idea what he was signing."

"My God, and you hold him!" Clara said, aghast. "How savage. Primitive!"

"Beg pardon, ma'am," Ben Cohen told her, "but he's a natural-born soldier, Holzer is. He loves it here, and he does a damned fine job. When he understands what's expected, that is. But like I said, he don't have much English, mostly Deutsch."

"That is no problem," Schotte said. "My own German is not too good, but I can count in the language. I shall understand the man well enough—if he's as reliable as you say."

"Very reliable, sir," Cohen assured him. He looked at Conway, who nodded.

"Malone and Holzer will do, Sergeant. Please advise them to be ready after morning grub."

"Excuse me, sir," Schotte said impatiently. "I will be leaving the outpost long before . . . grub," he spoke the word as if it tasted bad. "We want to be at the feeding grounds by sunrise. Have the men report to me at four in the morning, Sergeant."

Cohen looked to Captain Conway, who shrugged and nodded.

"Very good, sir," Cohen answered. "Now if you'll permit me to show you to your quarters—"

"The visiting officer's quarters?" Schotte asked.

"Why, yes, sir."

"Don't bother to show us, Sergeant," he said, shouldering his bag. "We can find our quarters. These army posts are designed, after all, with an unvarying similitude."

Ben Cohen shrugged and watched as the two went out, his eyes trailing them. When the outside door closed, he turned to Captain Conway, who was sitting, chin in hand, a bemused smile on his lips. Fitzgerald was grinning openly.

"Did you know that, sir?" Cohen asked.

"What's that, Sergeant?"

"That Number Nine had an unvarying similitude—I'll have to have that shined up right away."

Cohen held his straight face, but Fitzgerald barked a laugh. Cohen turned and strode to the office door, but then paused and asked, "What shall I tell Holzer and Malone they'll be doing, sir? So they'll know what equipment to take."

Warner Conway waved a hand and leaned back in his chair. "They won't need much but their horses, Sergeant. They'll just be counting humpies."

Ben Cohen's face expanded thoughtfully, then he cocked his head as if that could help him understand. "Beg pardon?"

"Counting humpies, Sergeant. Humpies. Damn, Ben, can't you hear?"

"Yes, sir, I hear you now. Sorry, sir!" He turned sharply and went into the orderly room, muttering to himself. Then Conway could hold the straight face no longer and he laughed out loud, Fitzgerald joining him. They repeated to each other, "Humpies!" and broke out again into laughter until the tears rolled down both men's cheeks.

five —————————————

Ben Cohen had swooped down like a tiger on fresh
meat upon the two new privates who had escorted Captain
Conway's party. Which was what they were to Ben
Cohen—fresh meat. He had learned long ago that the only
way to handle the job of first soldier was to come on hard
and loud. They could stay in line or they could step out past
the deadline—and after stepping beyond the deadline with
Ben Cohen, there were few who didn't toe the line.

There were a few who didn't take the bluff and went for
the thunder—like Dillson. Cohen frowned at that thought.
But Cohen was equipped with both bluff and thunder, which
he wielded with equal efficiency, and for good reason. They
didn't have to like him, but they had to respect him. It was
simple, really—if the men got out of line, Ben Cohen
looked bad in the officers' eyes, and he couldn't afford that.

Archer was a tall, sallow-complexioned soldier who had
done two years on his hitch already. He took Cohen's wel-
coming speech without expression, noting it, but hardly
trembling in his boots. There was a good reason for that.
Hale Archer had seen his share of first soldiers, knew they
had to come on tough, and he intended to do a job for
Cohen, stay out of trouble, and ride out his hitch.

It would have been better if Cohen had caught Archer

and Duckworth together. Then the younger private could have seen that Archer took it impersonally, that in fact Cohen meant nothing personal by it. It was his set speech, spoken loudly and warningly to every new man at Outpost Number Nine.

Duckworth had just finished putting his horse into the paddock and was bent over collecting his gear when Cohen found him.

The big shadow fell across Duckworth, and he glanced up with apprehension. He had been in the army three short months. He had never been away from his fatherless home before enlisting, and he was acutely aware of his small stature.

Wanting to do everything right, Duckworth came instantly to attention, snapped a salute, and said, "Good morning, sir!"

Ben Cohen's eyes opened wider and he assumed his stance, a sort of relaxed parade rest in which he bent forward from the waist and peered directly into the recruit's eyes.

"Don't ever call me 'sir,'" Cohen said in what was nearly a whisper but grew rapidly to a bull roar. "I am not 'sir,' I am *Sergeant* Cohen. Your first sergeant, soldier. You will address me as Sergeant Cohen, and never as 'sir.' Do you understand me?"

Duckworth was absolutely trembling. The big NCO in front of him dwarfed the soldier and intimidated him.

"Well!"

"Yes, Sergeant!" Duckworth answered.

"I want to welcome you to Easy Company, Duckworth," Cohen intoned. "If you keep your mouth shut and your ears open, you'll find us firm but fair. If you fuck up, you can give your soul to Jesus, because your ass will belong to me! I am Sergeant Cohen and I am the first soldier. When I say froggy I expect you to jump. If you think you can whip me I'll be glad to take off my stripes and show you the error of your ways. If you're ready to soldier, go over to the kitchen and tell them I said to coffee and grub you before

52

you report to your squad leader."

Duckworth's ears had gone to a burning crimson, and his mouth was dry. Now, he decided, he had had it. The first shirt had taken an instant dislike to him, even threatened to beat him up. This was going to be one miserable tour of duty.

"Any questions, Duckworth?"

"I don't . . . who is my squad leader?" he asked so softly that Ben couldn't hear him at first.

"Who is what?" Cohen boomed.

"My squad leader, sir?"

"Sir . . . Jesus." Ben wiped a hand over his face. "Report to Corporal Wojensky, he'll line you out." Duckworth still didn't move. "He's in the enlisted barracks, soldier."

Duckworth nodded, bent over to pick up his saddle, came again to attention, and finally walked off. Ben Cohen muttered a soft oath and watched the man go, wondering what barrel they were scraping to find these soldiers.

Duckworth's ears were still a flaming red when he reached the barracks. He tossed his saddle on the boardwalk, not knowing what the procedure was supposed to be. Then he stepped inside, looking warily around.

Three men were playing cards at the half-moon table abutting the back wall, and another soldier, wearing his boots, pants, and suspenders over a long underwear shirt, sat propped up on his bunk, hands behind his head, smoking.

"I'm looking for Corporal Wojensky," Duckworth said softly.

"Fresh meat?" the man on the bed asked around his half-cigar.

"Pardon me?"

The soldier on the bed sat up and repeated his question, forming it differently. "Are you assigned here or passing through?"

"I'm assigned to Easy Company. Duckworth's my name."

"Duckworth?" the man on the bed smiled faintly. He

53

looked rough to Duckworth, although he wasn't overly big. He had scarred hands showing a broken knuckle or two, and there was a devil-may-care gleam in his eyes. He was clean-shaven, but the shave wasn't recent and it shadowed his angular face.

"I'm Malone," the soldier said, offering a hand without rising. "You want to stay on Cohen's good side, it's probably best to stay away from me."

Duckworth had had his hand extended. Malone's joking comment caused his hand to falter, and he looked quickly into Malone's eyes to see if the man had noticed his hesitation. He had. There was a cynical amusement reflected there. They shook hands anyway, Duckworth's grip as firm as he could make it.

"That bunk's empty—no it ain't, Archer got it. Well—" Malone rubbed his jaw. "Those two over there by the door. They're drafty, that's why they're available. Take your choice."

Duckworth nodded his thanks and turned that way. The door swung open and three other soldiers tramped in from out of the brilliant sunlight. One of them was a huge man, his face puffy and cruel. He looked Duckworth up and down, and spat.

"Takin' 'em pint-sized now, ain't they!"

Duckworth's face flushed scarlet, and Dillson piled it on. "Hell, he blushes too, just like a woman!"

He laughed harshly and a quiet voice muttered, "Why don't you shut up, Dillson."

Dillson spun around, his fists clenching. Malone was propped up on his bed, hands behind his head, smoke dead in his lips. "Who asked you to butt in, Malone?"

"Who the hell asked *you* to?" Malone countered. "You're all mouth, nothin' but a pain in the ass since you got here. Shut up your damned cannon mouth, artillery boy, and leave the kid alone."

Duckworth tried to fade into the wall, his head swiveling from one man to the other.

54

"You scare me, Malone," Dillson said, taking a step toward him. "Look, I'm all atremble."

"I'm not trying to scare you, fat butt. I'm just tellin' you to keep your damned mouth shut. If you can't, I figure I can shut it for you."

"By God, I'll—" Dillson started to whip his coat off, but before he could get started, Wojensky, Rafferty, and Reb McBride stepped into the barracks, finished with their coffee and doughnuts from Rothausen's kitchen.

Wojensky saw the friction immediately and said, "Not in my barracks, boys. Jesus, Malone, haven't you had enough of barracks confinement?"

"I've had enough," Malone answered, "cooped up with the likes of that asshole."

Dillson stiffened again and started for Malone, but Corporal Wojensky grabbed his arm. "I'll have you on report too, Dillson. By God, I wouldn't think you'd want to see Sergeant Cohen again!"

"Just tell Malone to keep his damn mouth shut," Dillson said. He was trembling with anger, and Rafferty and Reb exchanged a look.

Dillson turned sharply and stamped out, banging the door behind him. Malone grinned and Reb told him, "Don't fuck with that man, Malone. Jesus! He's going to kill somebody someday."

"I'm tired of his bellyaching," Malone said. "He was giving the kid a hard time." He shrugged and crossed the room, watching the card game, which had begun again now that a promising fight had been halted.

Wojensky turned his eyes now to the new recruit. "You Duckworth?" he asked.

"Yes, Corporal."

Wojensky looked the little man over and nodded. "All right. I guess you've gotten Cohen's welcome-to-Number-Nine speech. I'll give you my own. Outside the barracks, I'm Corporal Wojensky. Inside or in town, I'm Wo."

"Glad to meet you," Duckworth said, extending his hand,

trying a timid smile. Wojensky mentally counted personnel and told him, "You'll be in Miller's squad, I guess. That'll put you with your friend Archer."

"He could be in our squad," Malone said from across the room. "We're a man short."

"Yeah, you," Wojensky replied. "Okay, you can be in my squad—Reb's handling it since I'm moving up to platoon sergeant temporarily. Duckworth, I'll give you the choice. If you want to stick with Archer, I'll hand you over to Miller."

Duckworth glanced at Malone, who nodded, and then back to Wojensky. "I'll stick with your squad if it's all right."

"Fine. This is Corporal McBride, our bugler, your temporary squad leader. This other man is Rafferty. Don't play cards with him. That's Malone, I guess you've met him. The stringbean in the corner is Dobbs, call him Stretch. That's Jefferson, with the chips in front of him, and . . . Wolfgang Holzer."

Holzer stood stiffly, clicked his heels, and bowed from the neck before taking his seat again at the card table.

"And if you need anything—"

The door swung open behind Wojensky, and he turned. Ben Cohen stood there, scowling. "What the hell's going on in here? I just saw Dillson slam this door and stalk off." Ben tested the door. Surprisingly, it was still hung right.

"Think he had some indigestion," Malone said, walking over.

"If he did, I can imagine who gave it to him. Look, I know the man's a pain in the ass. Please, though, get along with him until I can get him shipped back to artillery. I'd hate to have to bust somebody over him." He paused. Duckworth was busily unpacking. "Everything all right, Duckworth?"

"Fine, sir."

Cohen winced. "All right. Malone, turn in early tonight. At four *a.m.*, you are to report to a Dr. Schotte. He's in the visiting officers' quarters."

56

"Four! Jesus, Sarge."

"Four, Private."

"I thought I was restricted to barracks."

"That's over. Captain Conway's orders. You got a break, Malone. Don't blow this. Holzer is going with you. Sometime between now and then, somebody please figure out how to get that information to him."

Holzer's head had come up at the mention of his name and he started to rise. Cohen waved him back into his chair.

"Why can't someone teach that man English?"

"He's working on it, Sergeant. He's got a book he studies every night."

"Really?" Cohen was suitably impressed. "Good, that'll be one less problem around here." He raised his voice. "You learning English, Holzer?"

"Quite defectively!" Holzer shouted back. "From these scotch books."

Cohen shook his head, not bothering to try deciphering that. "Keep at it," he said with waning optimism. To Malone he said, "Four o'clock."

"Mind telling me what we'll be doing?" Malone asked.

"Counting humpies, Private."

Malone blinked. He felt like Holzer. Was everyone going to doubletalk around here? "Sergeant?" he said. "Did you say—?"

"Humpies. Dammit, Malone, humpies!"

Cohen was not smiling, so Malone didn't, but he stood there running it through his mind as Cohen walked out the door, closing it carefully behind him. Malone sat on his bunk, still musing.

He glanced at Reb and said, *"Humpies,* did he say? Counting *humpies?"*

"So to work the humpies," Holzer said, nodding with satisfaction. Malone looked at Holzer, his face blank.

"Did *he* understand that?" Malone asked Wojensky.

Holzer had picked up a third eight to go with his pair, and he raked in the pot triumphantly, smiling at Malone, who sagged back on his bunk, Cohen's words circling his mind, finding no definition. "Guess I'll find out in the mornin'," he said to no one in particular. Then he closed his eyes, listening to the rising wind whistling through the chinks in the barracks walls.

Second Lieutenant Taylor had just come off twenty-four hours of OD. He lay motionless on his bunk, snoring melodiously as Matt Kincaid returned to quarters, his spirits high.

"Wake up, Mr. Taylor," Matt said, shaking the sleeping officer's shoulder.

"Nawagh mup," Taylor grumbled, rolling over.

"Ah, but you have to wake up," Kincaid said, sitting on Taylor's bunk.

"Frwat?" Taylor muttered sleepily.

"There's been a war while you slept. The Cheyenne Nation has defeated the United States. Crazy Horse has been elected President of the United Indian Nation, and to balance the ticket he chose Jefferson Davis as his vice-president. I, fortunately, have been chosen governor of Wyoming—which is now known as Buffalo Dung." He shook Taylor's shoulder again, grinning. "Are you awake, Taylor?"

"I am now." Taylor slid his feet to the floor and scratched his head. "I think I am, that is. What time is it, Matt?"

"One-thirty."

"Jesus, I did sleep. Captain back?"

"He is. And, I might add, he has produced a summer-replacement officer. Meaning," Matt said, slapping Taylor's shoulder, "that the second-in-command is now free to depart for Denver."

"Don't want to change your mind?"

"Fitzgerald already tried that. No, I don't want to switch furlough time."

"It'll be awful damned hot in Denver. Maybe next month . . . I was just thinking of you, Matt."

"And I'm thinking of you. I'll go now, while it's hot. *You* enjoy the coolness next month."

Taylor rose and walked to the washbasin, and poured

58

water into it. He splashed his face and ran his fingers through his hair.

"Fitz came back all right, then."

"He lost two soldiers," Matt Kincaid told him. "Three more nicked. Gus Olsen was hit, but he's doing all right now. Maggie Cohen's mothering him."

"The new man—a shavetail?" Taylor inquired. He had slipped into his tunic and stood buttoning it.

"Yes. But he's married, brought his wife along. By the way, I'd break out my dress blues if I were you. Dinner with the captain and the missus tonight."

Taylor stared at him with sleepy frustration. "You could have told me before I put this on."

"Slipped my mind, Taylor," Matt said cheerfully. He had gotten into his locker and was throwing articles onto the bunk. "Everything seems to be slipping my mind right now. As I slip away from Number Nine." His hand described a gesture of slipping away.

"Damn," Taylor said. His voice was spiritless, "I wish to God I was slipping away." He mimicked Matt's gesture.

"Soon enough, Mr. Taylor. Rank does have its privileges, after all."

"I mean it, Matt," he said soberly. "I think I'm getting High Plains fever."

"That something like cabin fever?" Matt asked, producing a brand-new black leather satchel that Taylor had never seen before.

"Exactly," Taylor answered. He crossed to his own locker and stood eyeing his dress blues morosely. "Except you add a few hostiles, a cold north wind, and six million buffalo pies."

"This is a side of you I've never seen, Taylor. Always saw you as an intrepid warrior, rugged frontiersman, and all."

"I'm serious, Matt," Taylor said, turning toward him. "Damn place is getting to me. First you go, then Fitz—I should have called heads—then, if there's anything left of me, I'll go."

"You are serious."

"I am."

Matt Kincaid frowned thoughtfully and turned away, packing his satchel, carefully placing his orders in an inside pocket. "Your turn will come soon enough, Taylor. You going to Denver like everyone else?" he asked conversationally.

"Kansas City, Matt. I told you, Kansas City."

"I'd forgotten."

Taylor sat in a backward-turned chair, facing Kincaid, and told him, "There's a place there that has oysters and stuffed mushrooms, Matt. Stuffed with truffles. The Fontainebleau, it's called."

"I never knew you were a gourmet."

"I'm not. Or I never was. But it's a funny thing. The closer my furlough gets, the more I think about the Fontainebleau. Stuffed mushrooms—I see them in my sleep. I think I'm going crazy." Taylor sat quietly, his head resting on the back of the chair. Suddenly he brightened. "I know what you can do for me, Matt!"

"I'm not switching furloughs," Matt replied with a grin.

"Not that." Taylor stood and walked excitedly to where Matt was packing. "There's something else that's been on my mind. It's driving me crazy thinking about it. I stay awake at nights."

"I can't bring a woman back, Taylor."

Taylor smiled faintly. "No, not that. But there is something you can bring me, Matt. If you would."

"Of course. What is it?"

Taylor's eyes were bright, and he reached over and rested a hand on Matt Kincaid's shoulder. For a startling moment, Matt considered the possibility that Taylor *was* slightly off his rocker. His eyes positively glittered. He said in a low, conspiratorial voice:

"Otard-Dupuy."

Matt blinked, his face blank. "What?"

"Otard-Dupuy VSOP brandy. 1837."

"You want a bottle of brandy?"

"Not brandy, Matt. The nectar of the gods, the elysian essence."

"You *are* all right, aren't you?" Matt asked uncertainly.

"Of course I'm all right! I will be, if you promise to bring me a quart of Otard-Dupuy. I'll write down the name of a shop."

"Don't bother, I can remember it," Matt said.

"No. I'm not taking any chances." He scribbled something down and dug into his duffle, withdrawing a small buckskin pouch. He handed Matt five gold eagles.

"Fifty dollars! Two months' pay for a bottle of brandy?"

"It's more than that, Matt. More than a bottle of brandy. It's salvation. Fifty dollars—I'd pay a hundred. But it has to be 1837, Matt. I wrote it down there."

Matt shrugged and slipped the eagles into his satchel. "If it makes me happy, anything."

"It does make me happy," Taylor said, rubbing his hands together gleefully. "Otard-Dupuy." He sighed. "Ah!"

Matt smiled. Maybe old Taylor was popping a few buttons. If he was, Catha Haversham would completely undo him. She was undoubtedly the most perfectly beautiful woman Matt had ever seen, and he had seen some. He decided to save her as a surprise for Taylor.

Later, when Taylor asked, "You say this Haversham brought his wife—what's she look like, Matt?" Matt told him:

"She's a very intelligent woman, well schooled, friendly."

"Oh," Taylor said significantly. When they were described as intelligent and friendly, they had to be dogs. Matt was grinning, but Taylor supposed he was thinking about Denver again, and didn't press it. He put Mrs. Haversham out of his thoughts and finished dressing, thinking only of the Otard-Dupuy.

six _____

Flora Conway wore a dazzling smile and a black dress with lace cuffs when she opened the door for Kincaid and Taylor. She welcomed them and looked out the door for Fitzgerald before remembering that despite having just ridden in, he had drawn officer-of-the-day duty.

Flora closed the door behind them, took both their arms, and walked them into her parlor, which was not a separate room, but an area Flora had set aside for her social functions and where she had placed her prized red velvet settee and matching chair.

Sergeant Ben Cohen was there, sitting to one side, uneasily balancing a fragile teacup and saucer on his big knee. It was unusual for Cohen to be invited, and he suspected— correctly—that he had been included so that Maggie might attend.

Warner Conway, impeccable in his dress blues, rose to shake hands. Taylor shook the captain's hand and then stopped, transfixed.

She sat there in quiet radiance, her dark hair swept back from her perfect face, exposing small pink ears. Her eyes were dark beneath arched, tapering eyebrows. Her mouth was full, sensuous.

Taylor became suddenly aware that the others were simply watching him. Matt Kincaid was smiling insufferably.

"You haven't met Mrs. Haversham, have you?" Captain Conway asked. "And this, of course, is Mr. Haversham, our summer-replacement officer, whom I know you will be pleased to welcome."

"It is a pleasure," Taylor said, taking Catha's hand rather stiffly, then turning to shake hands with Everett Haversham.

"Over here, dear Mr. Taylor," Flora said. She stood behind an available chair, her smile enigmatic.

"Thank you, Mrs. Conway," Taylor said. He shot Matt Kincaid an accusing glance. The man could at least have warned him. *Intelligent. Friendly.* My God, the woman was perfect! He tried not to notice her figure, but it was difficult. She wore a beige dress that plunged recklessly at the neckline, revealing the swelling curves of smooth, firm breasts. Taylor swiveled in his chair and determinedly faced his commanding officer, who was addressing Haversham.

"We have two civilian visitors to the outpost. I invited Dr. Schotte and his assistant to dinner, but they declined. I believe the man has a repugnance for comfort."

"What is it you said they were doing?" Catha Haversham inquired.

"Counting... buffalo, Catha." He had paused, and in that pause Matt and Warner Conway had exchanged a glance. Matt smiled. *Humpies.*

"I think the man's off-center," Matt said.

"It seems impossible, this counting," Taylor agreed.

"The Department of the Interior has come up with another grand, impossible, and costly scheme, it seems," Conway said with a trace of bitterness.

"I don't know," Catha put in. "It could be quite useful. After all, no one knows how many buffalo there are. One hears that there are millions, but that means nothing. Are there enough to waste? Enough to feed the Indians? Perhaps there is actually a surplus."

"Stated in that way, it does seem a noble enterprise," Warner Conway admitted. "It's just that I have seen so many ridiculous bureaucratic experiments. It may indeed have value, but the idea of one little man wandering the Plains attempting it—absurd."

"Pathetic, in a way," Catha agreed. Her husband looked at her devotedly. Taylor watched with simple amazement. Her voice was clear, cadenced, neither hysterical nor strident, neither too modulated nor timid. She continued, "From another perspective, it is quite noble. The job is vast, his resources limited. I can imagine they've endured quite a lot. Did you say they've spent eighteen months, mostly in the open, struggling to complete this task? And his assistant is a young woman! I find it remarkable, don't you, Flora?"

"Well, yes," she answered, as if that point of view weren't new to that moment. "It is remarkable, I suppose. I just hadn't thought of it."

"Dr. Schotte is a remarkable man," Captain Conway said without inflection. "We have time for a drink before dinner, gentlemen, don't we, Maggie? May I pour?"

"Thank you," Haversham replied. Matt nodded and Taylor stood to walk with Conway to the sideboard where his liquor was stored.

"Sergeant Cohen?"

Cohen glanced up, still uncomfortably balancing the dainty teacup. He looked at the tea, which he had not tasted, and answered, "If I might, sir."

"Maggie!" Captain Conway said across his shoulder. "I think your husband's finished with his tea."

With obvious relief, Ben Cohen handed the cup to Maggie and, straightening his tunic, turned to join the officers at the sideboard.

Conway poured bourbon all around and replaced the crystal carafe. "Welcome to you and Mrs. Haversham," the captain toasted, raising his glass.

"I thank you," the second lieutenant said. "You are making us feel welcome indeed. Tomorrow," Haversham said to Taylor, "I understand you and Lieutenant Fitzgerald will be able to give me a tour of the area. The Indian agency included."

"Yes. We'll give you an opportunity to meet your first Cheyenne up close."

"Good. I'm really eager to begin."

"No more eager than I am to have you begin. The rotation in our officer-of-the-day schedule is fouled up. Inspections are months behind schedule."

"And the fighting, sir?" Haversham asked, a bit more eagerly than Captain Conway would have expected.

"We are always ahead of schedule there, Mr. Haversham" he said wryly. He finished his drink and nodded toward the table. "The ladies, it appears, are ready to dine."

Before seating themselves, Conway took Haversham aside and told him bluntly, "Mr. Haversham, you are needed badly on this outpost. It has been a long while since any of my officers has been free to take furlough. But please understand me, your utility lies on post and not in the field. I do not think it would be possible to train a field officer in the length of time you will have with us, and I do not intend to have a summer-replacement officer killed out here. It makes it damnably hard to get anyone next year."

"I understand." The disappointment was obvious on young Haversham's face. Perhaps he had had visions of himself leading the charge against hordes of painted, feathered savages. "Nevertheless," he said brightly, "I'm sure this will be a valuable experience for me. I have every intention of enjoying a long career. Who knows, sir—one day I may return as a regular officer."

Together they walked to the table, where Kincaid and Taylor stood behind their chairs, waiting. Conway and Haversham held their ladies' chairs out and Cohen belatedly followed suit, causing Maggie to break into a smile. The big first sergeant was obviously miserable in this unaccustomed situation.

Supper was something he could enjoy, however; it was Maggie Cohen's justly famous pot roast served with real fresh potatoes and not those damned "dessicated spuds." There was dark, rich gravy and Flora had made oven warm,

65

yeasty bread—it was slathered with fresh butter, probably bought for this occasion and paid for dearly from the sutler, Pop Evans.

Dessert was a cheesecake, one of Flora's specialties. Light and delicious. After dinner they relaxed at the table with coffee until the captain adjourned the gathering to the parlor, where he again offered drinks all around.

It was after they had finished their first drinks and Conway had poured a second that Catha suggested, "If it is at all possible, Captain Conway, I should very much like to visit the Indian agency too."

"I'm afraid there isn't much to see," Warner Conway answered with a smile.

"No." She laughed. "I realize that. You forget, I come from a place not so very different. But there are *people* there, and that is where my interest lies."

"Are you referring to your thoughts on civilizing these Indians, dear?" Flora asked.

"Yes, of course." Catha's face reflected genuine surprise.

"It's not just a notion with Catha," Everett Haversham put in. Kincaid and Taylor had no idea what he was talking about, so Haversham explained, "Catha thinks that the hostiles, in time, could be made to realize that their fight is hopeless, and that it is in their best interests to adopt the white man's civilized culture, as the Cherokee have done." Haversham looked at his wife with quiet pride. Sergeant Cohen nearly choked on his drink.

Catha said, "I can read it in your eyes, Captain. Another lost if noble cause, like the buffalo counting."

"I wouldn't put it so strongly, Catha. But I simply disagree with you. You don't know the Cheyenne. Believe me, nothing but the sword can induce them to surrender or alter their way of life."

"But you haven't tried," Catha said imploringly. "I can speak to them—as one Indian to another."

"A Cherokee is no more a friend to the Cheyenne than a white man, Catha," Kincaid felt obliged to put in. "The tribal enmities are strong. Anyone not of the tribe is against

66

it, and is therefore the enemy. It's always been that way."

"Except when there is something to be gained," she countered. They looked at her blankly. "Why," she explained, "look at Wraps-Up-His-Tail. A Crow medicine man who had gathered Sioux and Arapaho to fight. They listened to him."

"If he had preached peace, they wouldn't have," Taylor said.

"But you can't know that," she protested. Her dark eyes were thoughtful for a moment. "To forestall bloodshed you had to resort to bloodshed yourself. I have a foot in both worlds, Captain Conway. I understand them; I want no one to be killed. If they only understood. And I can be useful out here. All Indians are brothers. If the Cherokee can benefit from modernization, so can the Cheyenne—if only it is presented to them logically."

The girl was so intent, so goodhearted, that Conway didn't wish to argue with her any further. He simply told her, "We have certain rules on the outpost, Catha. I know you don't want to violate any of them and see your husband get into trouble. I want you to promise me you will obey these rules."

"I will," she said, looking slightly puzzled.

"Fine. One of the rules is that no woman is to leave this outpost unescorted."

"But—" She started to argue, but Conway held up a hand.

"You must adhere to that rule. As to seeing the Indian agency, I think that will be all right. Perhaps your husband can take you there one day when he is off duty, after he has learned a little more about the area himself. You may speak with the Indians there all you wish—if they will listen. But as far as being a peacemaker, seeking out hostile Cheyenne—you'll have to lay that idea to rest right now, Catha. Do you understand me?"

"I understand the rules, yes," she replied softly, "but not the thinking behind them. They are hostiles; we are hostiles to them. No one speaks, we only kill."

Her words were spoken with such feeling that Conway was unable to argue with the girl any longer. He only looked to Flora. Perhaps a woman could explain matters a little better.

He himself thought glumly of the unfortunate women he had found mutilated and murdered by the hostiles, of those who had been raped before the eyes of their husbands or children. Those hostiles had had little inclination to talk things over, to become "civilized."

When the others had gone and they were undressing for bed, Warner Conway talked it over with his wife.

"I hope," he told Flora as he unfastened her dress for her, "our young Mrs. Haversham will come to realize the folly of attempting to put her ideas into practice."

"I'm sure she will." Flora kissed her husband's forehead and carefully hung up the black dress. "When Mr. Haversham has learned enough to tell her some of the gruesome tales we all have heard, it will give her pause to consider."

"I wonder." Warner Conway exerted a little more pressure on the bootjack and his right boot popped off. "She dominates the man, it seems to me. Not in any conscious or evil way, of course, but he is wholly devoted to her. Her physical attributes seem to have Mr. Haversham quite in awe."

"I wish I had that power over you," Flora teased, folding her petticoats. Conway's eyes lifted to her laughing eyes and then swept pleasurably down her still-beautiful body.

"Why, you do, Flora," he told her. "But I suppose I am too old to be altogether foolish about it."

"You find young Mr. Haversham foolish?"

"Foolish is not the right word, I suppose." Warner stood, unbuckled his trousers, and removed them. "More blinded. Infatuated, perhaps. He dotes on her beauty, positively basks in her glow. He enjoys presenting her to other men, watching their eyes."

"He is proud of Catha, that's all."

"I don't mean any of this to sound petty," Captain Conway replied. "I suppose it does, in a way. I simply mean that he takes inordinate pride in her beauty, in saying, 'See what I have.' It is an immature attitude, though hardly uncommon."

"They are young and in love, Warner." Flora came to him, placing her hands on his chest. He kissed her warmly. "As we were."

"As we *were!*" he said with mock gruffness. "By God, we're as much in love as ever. More than ever." He held her to him, and she smiled.

"But not so young."

"No. And that doesn't matter either. That's perhaps a part of what I am trying to say, Flora. Our love doesn't depend on holding hands in the moonlight, on my being enraptured with your beauty. It endures because I see all of you, love all of you. I only worry that Mr. Haversham places too much emphasis on Catha's beauty."

"I'm sure that's not all he sees in her, Warner. She is clever, devoted to him, goodhearted—idealistic, if you will, but compassionate."

"I want you to promise me you will talk to her again," Warner Conway said.

Flora looked mildly surprised. "Of course I will. If you think it necessary."

"I don't know if it is or not. I just want to be sure. Many idealists are harmless, if silly—but if the girl really clings to this idea that it is all right for her to ride out there and speak to the hostiles because they are her 'brothers,' it is far from a harmless preoccupation. I want you to impress that on her."

"I shall." They still clung together, and the lantern was burning low. "But for now I want to impress myself upon you."

"You're shameless," he said, kissing her nose, her bare shoulder.

"Quite." She kissed his throat, and her hands stroked his strong, bare back. "It took you quite a bit of effort to convince me that a properly reared Maryland lady would do some of the things you like to do, Warner."

"But I convinced you." His hand cupped her still-firm, full breasts and his lips lowered to administer three gentle lingering kisses.

"Yes." Her voice was breathy. "But you don't want me backsliding, do you?" She stood silently, head back, feeling his lips move across her breasts, linger on her throat. "I does take practice, dear. Practice, practice, practice..."

He scooped her up and carried her to the bed and laid her down on it, then leaned over the bed table and blew out the lamp. In a moment he had slipped between the cool sheets to find her waiting there, breathless, eager.

They lay side by side, her soft breathing gentle against his ear. He kissed her forehead, her cheek, her moist lips, and let his hands travel the familiar but always new curves of her body—the rise of her hips, the tapering line of her thighs. She kissed his chest and let her head loll back. Her hair spread against the pillow and she stroked his arm with her fingertips, studying his strong face as his hands awakened her desire.

She rolled away from him, resting on her back, and as his hands lingered on the soft inner flesh of her thighs, her legs parted to his inspection. Flora closed her eyes, letting sensation dominate her thoughts. In the darkness he was warm and strong and she opened to him, letting his fingers toy with her, bringing her emotions to the surface.

She was damp now, and it was warm in the night. Flora put her forearm across her eyes and her other hand dropped between her thighs to meet his. Their fingers intertwined and she felt her own juices on his fingers. He guided her hand with his own, and together they strove to bring her to a peak of sensation.

Warner's hand rested on top of hers, dipping inside as she stroked herself, feeling a loosening, a quivering within. A flash of light danced through her brain and a humming sound filled her ears.

Slipping her hand from under his, she reached for him and found him hard, erect and pulsing. Her thumb traced

70

gentle, maddening whorls across the head of his erection, and her fingers stroked his shaft lightly.

She rolled to him, hearing his heart drumming inside his broad chest. His erection was against the soft flesh of her belly and she brushed it slowly back and forth against her as her free hand cupped his taut pouch.

She enjoyed cradling the round heft of his sack in her palm. Often, at times like this, she thought longingly of what lay within him there—the seed to begin a child within her. Her heart quickened as that thought mingled with the excitement she already rode.

Almost lazily, Flora disengaged herself and rolled onto her stomach, spreading her legs still wider. Warner got to his knees and kissed her back between the shoulder blades, kissed the white fullness of her buttocks, her inner thighs, pungent with her earthy woman-scent.

Then, resting his hands on her buttocks, he eased up behind her, watching her face, which was turned to one side on the pillow, a deep, contented smile on her mouth as he reached between her legs, parted her with his thumbs, and slid the head of his shaft just inside of her warmth.

He paused there, feeling the tiny clutchings of the muscles within Flora. He saw her lift herself slightly and saw her arm move. Then he felt her hand between her legs, stroking him lazily, drawing him gently in.

He entered her fully, feeling her flesh surround him, feeling her fingers clutch his balls and hold him there, locked against her as her hips lifted and held perfectly still.

Then her hand fell away and she thrust her hips higher, getting to her knees as he knelt behind her, his hands against her buttocks, feeling the rippling of the muscles that lay beneath the soft layer of feminine fat.

Flora's face was contorted with emotion. She might almost have been in agony—her eyes were shut so tightly that lines rayed out from them. Her brow was corrugated, her jaw sagged open; one knuckle was pressed against her teeth.

71

She might have been in agony but for the way her fluid hips rose and fell, demanding more. They swayed rhythmically and then not so rhythmically as Flora climbed a ladder of sensuality to its highest rung before toppling off into the bottomless joy beyond.

He felt her tense, come undone, felt the rippling of tiny muscles against him, the damp release, and it brought Warner Conway to an intense need. He ground his pelvis against the soft cushions of her buttocks. Leaning forward unsteadily he found her breasts with his hands and clung to her, his body moving jerkily in an almost uncontrollable series of bucking thrusts until he could hold it back no longer and he came with a rush before falling against her and lying there quietly, stroking her dark hair as the night slipped away and their hearts fell to a slow, regular beating.

Rafferty had drawn guard duty that night, a night that started out mild and clear after a long hot day, but had grown progressively colder until after midnight it was bitterly cold, and the guards were forced to break out their greatcoats.

At three-thirty the stars stood large and brilliant against a black velvet sky. The outpost was dark and silent, as silent as the sky and the black plains over the palisade.

Rafferty reported to the watch sergeant and got permission to leave his post. He climbed down the rough ladder, his hands stiff with the cold, breath fogging from his lips as he missed a step and barked a shin on the ladder.

Crossing to the barracks, he stepped inside, the faint warmth of the building at this hour like a hot summer wind after the outdoors. He crossed to Malone's bunk, prodded him, and stepped back. The man had been known to come flying out of that bed, fists swinging, especially after a night's drinking.

This time, Malone merely rolled over, lifted one heavy eyelid, and struggled to make out the figure in the darkened room.

"Malone, get up."

"Rafferty?"

"Yes."

"Get fucked."

"You got to get up. Special detail."

"What time is it?" Malone asked from out of the stupor of heavy sleep.

"Three-thirty."

"Jesus." There was a long silence as Malone's conscious mind slowly came alert. He muttered, "I had to be a god-damn soldier."

Rafferty, bundled so that he could hardly move in gloves, greatcoat, and muffler, moved to Wolfgang Holzer's bunk. This was an easier task.

He touched Holzer's shoulder and the man sat up instantly, nearly at attention.

"Three-thirty," Rafferty said, and Holzer nodded, coming to his feet, dressing as rapidly as possible. Rafferty watched him with amazement. An army of Holzers, he reflected, could conquer the world. Assuming they all spoke the same language.

Malone was still sitting on the side of his bunk, head hanging, but he was up. Rafferty buttoned up against the cold and went back to the wall, first warning the two men that there was frost on the pumpkins.

Malone clawed at his sleep-crusted eyes, splashed water onto his face, and slowly, methodically dressed as Holzer stood by eagerly, already clad in greatcoat and hat.

"What's your hurry?" Malone wondered.

"Count the humpies," Holzer answered with enthusiasm.

"Yeah."

Holzer was just happy to be up and about. He had had his horse shot out from under him at Salt Creek. The horse had rolled onto Holzer's foot, snapping it at the ankle. He had lain abed for ten days, then spent a long convalescence helping Four Eyes with his clerking duties and mopping out the barracks.

Holzer still wasn't fit for a hard ride—the ankle couldn't take the strain. But this was a welcome duty for him after having been post-bound for nearly six weeks.

73

Bundled to their chins, they went out into the cold, clear night. The paddock was deserted and they cut out two horses. Holzer had found one horse that would stand for an off-side mount, and he claimed that one. He got his right foot into the stirrup and, with Malone's rough help, swung his injured leg over. He left that boot dangling free of the stirrup. Grinning, Holzer waited while Malone looped a hammerhead bay with a black tail. That horse, Malone knew, was hard-headed and enjoyed nipping at legs, but it was a runner, and Malone always made it a point to try to have a good horse under him when he was out on the plains.

Counting humpies or fighting, he wanted to be able to run if it came to that. After a dust-stirring battle with the bay, Malone saddled, slapping the horse's nose away as it tried to nip his thigh, and together they crossed the empty parade just as a pale, rising half moon whitened the stockade walls.

The two civilians were already mounted, waiting. The tall man was glancing at his watch impatiently, and he snapped at Malone.

"You're ten minutes late."

"Sorry," Malone said without a smile. "I woke up with a stiff pecker."

Schotte stiffened. "There's a lady present, soldier!"

Was there? Malone peered at the second civilian. A buffalo coat with a fur collar shrouded the figure. A flop hat with a ridiculous fur fringe covered the forehead, and all he could see of the face was a pair of spectacles glinting in the moonlight. He took Schotte's word for it.

"Sorry, ma'am."

"I've been warned you are a troublemaker, Malone. I'll have none of that on this expedition."

Malone regarded the doctor soberly. Then, ornately, he spat on the ground, touching his hatbrim. Holzer, unremarkably, was still grinning.

"And you are the Deutscher."

"To count the humpies!"

"Yes!" Schotte was encouraged. "Gad, boy, I like your eagerness."

"Yes," Holzer repeated, and Malone sighed, sitting far forward, hands braced on the saddlebow of his McClellan.

Schotte glanced again at his watch before tucking it away in the bulk of his hair coat. "We're already late. I want to catch the buffalo at first light when they're up for morning graze."

"Buffalo!" Malone said with sudden understanding. "We're going out to count buffalo!" He laughed sharply, and Schotte glared at him.

"If we may proceed," Dr. Schotte said stiffly.

"Please," Malone said with a flourish of his hand.

Schotte led the small party toward the gate, and it was swung wide to allow the four riders and a heavily laden packmule to exit.

They rode southward and then gradually east as the gray light along the horizon promised dawn. The land here gradually rose in a series of low hummocks. Cresting one of these, Dr. Schotte drew up. Malone could see him, black and motionless against the false dawn, frozen with excitement.

Drawing up beside Schotte, he saw the herd. Buffalo were scattered against the grass, dark mounds against the hardly lighter earth. They were barely moving, or at least Malone could detect no motion at this distance. Their smell was obvious, however.

"Fine, fine," Schotte said, his voice an electric whisper.

Dismounting, he walked to the packmule, with Malone watching him. He glanced at Holzer, who seemed every bit as eager as Schotte, and then at the other civilian—the girl, he supposed, but he had only Schotte's word on it as evidence.

She trembled slightly, whether with excitement or the chill of morning. Schotte had removed a bulky pack from the patient mule and he had his gear spread on the dark, frosted earth.

75

He stood as Malone, leading his horse, approached him. Malone watched as Schotte fitted one section of pole into another until he had a pike nearly fifteen feet long. A paintbrush was affixed to one end.

"What's that for?" Malone inquired. Schotte looked at him as if his patience were exhausted.

"Swatching, Private Malone."

"Swatching. Well, that's as obvious as 'humpies,' ain't it?"

"I find sarcasm tedious before dawn," Schotte replied tightly.

"Sorry—thought I was asking a simple question."

"Yes, I forget that you know nothing of scientific methodology. You see," Schotte explained, "I can't count the same humpie twice. So this is used to mark each animal." He opened a five-gallon can of whitewash. "Harmless to the bison, I assure you."

"You dab 'em with that long paintbrush."

"Quite."

"Beg pardon, but ain't that a little hazardous? A big bull will go maybe two thousand pounds, for Christ's sake!"

A buffalo may look placid and stupid, and they are, but roused or panicked, that's a lot of muscle and horn. Malone had seen buffalo commit mayhem against a pack of hungry wolves.

"What if they stampede?" he asked.

"Very hazardous in that case. That's why the beaters have to be most cautious."

"The beaters?"

"Yes, you and Holzer. Good beaters can be absolutely essential. The Zulu are among the best. When I was counting zebra in the Sudan—"

"We are supposed to get down there and herd them by you?" Malone asked incredulously.

"Yes, of course."

"Of course, hell. If they get to running, they'll trample our horses—and us, likely."

"Yes, yes, Malone," Schotte said with an exasperated

sigh. "Of course you can't use horses. That's why we've brought these."

He produced two rolled hides that Malone was able to identify as buffalo skins. "Just the ticket."

"You're crazy, Schotte."

"I beg your pardon! Hardly crazy, my dear Private Malone. I have been utilizing this method for eighteen months now. Learned it from the Indians. Put on a buffalo skin"—Schotte demonstrated, throwing the hide over his shoulders and head—"and you can slip right among the humpies."

"Good. Get yourself an Indian for this job. Or do it yourself. I'm damn sure not going to go down there. If them big bastards get to running, I'll be trampled so far into the mud that you won't be able to find Malone again."

"May I remind you that this is an official expedition? That your commanding officer has placed you at my disposal?"

"That's one I owe the captain," Malone said.

"Please, it's getting light already," Schotte said.

"Please, Private Malone," the woman said. She was a woman, apparently, or a man who had had a serious accident, judging by the small voice that rose out of the ruff of fur. "I assure you, it's not so hazardous as it seems. We've never lost a soldier yet."

Yet. Smothering a curse, Malone took the buffalo robe from Schotte, watching as Holzer did the same. Both robes were full hides, including the massive heads, which bobbed with every movement, threatening to topple them over. The feet dragged on the ground as they moved.

Malone was wondering if he had really awakened yet—this all seemed like some bizarre dream. He and Holzer, standing on that knoll like two Cheyenne medicine men ready to go down among the milling buffalo so that the good doctor could daub their butts with whitewash.

Malone glanced at Holzer, and he would have laughed aloud except for the growing uneasiness in his guts. Holzer stood erect, his eyes alert beneath the massive, stuffed head of a bull buffalo. Malone wondered if he looked just as ridiculous—he figured he must, and now he wanted only to get on with this.

Sunrise was streaking the low pennants of cloud along the eastern horizon with crimson and gold. Schotte was beside Malone, whispering, "We'll take up our station in that clump of brush alongside the wallow. You men start them walking that way. Slowly, man, slowly."

There was no need for the warning. Malone meant to do it all with infinite caution. He and Holzer worked down the draw and walked a long half-circle to the rear of the herd, coming up downwind. The buffalo apparently had no awareness of man-scent, but Malone certainly had his nostrils filled with buffalo scent. They were rank, shaggy, and wet from wallowing.

Glancing at Holzer, who had moved slightly to the west, Malone eased up toward the tail end of the herd. Stretching out a hand, he nudged his first buffalo, an old cow, and she took three steps and paused. He followed her forward, prodded her again, and got absolutely no result except for a slap of her tail in his face.

Since the buffalo seemed far from frightened of him and unlikely to stampede—in fact they seemed stupidly ignorant of his presence—Malone put both hands firmly on the haunches of the buffalo and shoved as hard as the muddy, dung-sloppy footing would allow. The cow calmly lifted her tail and dropped an offering at Malone's feet.

Smoldering, Malone gave that one up and moved to the west himself. Holzer, looking like an emaciated, side-hopping buffalo himself in the gray of morning, plodded along behind two buffalo he had somehow started into motion. As these nudged those feeding in front of them, they automatically moved along as well.

Malone moved among them, starting a few forward. A big bull rolled its tiny, lifeless eyes in his direction and then turned, its massive head wagging.

Malone froze. His heart skipped a beat. Perhaps the big bull thought this was a challenge from an upstart youngster.

78

Malone shifted away from the bull, which continued to eye him suspiciously.

Now the buffalo were actually funneling into the area of the wallow, where two knolls approached each other and narrowed the meadow. From time to time, Malone saw the white brush of Dr. Schotte stretch out and daub the flanks of the passing buffalo as they ambled forward.

Malone slapped a calf on the haunches and it started forward with a leap. Malone smiled until it turned. The calf's mother was behind him, her big head lowered, wagging from side to side.

Malone backed away and bumped right into the big bull, which had not forgotten this upstart for one moment. He turned slowly, finding the bull's eyes nearly at his own eye level.

There was dead grass in the bull's wooly coat, dung on its flank, and fire in its dull little eyes. Malone took a backward step and the buffalo charged.

There was no way to dodge it, nowhere to run, so Malone took the charge head-on. Fortunately the buffalo had little running start, but still the massive head of the animal slammed into Malone's chest with the force of a triphammer, knocking the breath from him, lighting up his head with colored lights that blinked on and off.

He had the presence of mind to hook his arms over the buffalo's horns, but there was nothing else he could do except yell, and he hollered for all he was worth as the buffalo, on a rampage now, bucked its head and charged across the meadow, with Malone in his buffalo-hide costume clinging desperately to the rolling, butting buffalo. He had hold of two thousand pounds of angry meat and horns, and no way to get free of it.

"Holzer! Holzer!" Malone bellowed, but there was nothing in the world that Holzer could do but stand gawking as the buffalo thundered by, trying to toss Malone, who was being flipped about as if he weighed nothing.

If he let go, he would be trampled. He thought desperately of his Schofield, but he had left his pistol with his horse, having no idea of needing it while counting buffalo. Even if he had it, it was doubtful he could draw the weapon, holding on with one hand, and dispatch the brawling bull.

The buffalo ran in a tight circle, changing tactics, and Malone was slammed into a second animal, knocking the wind from him violently. Then the bull stopped dead, abruptly, and Malone nearly swung free.

He clung to the horns, his arms nearly wrenched from their sockets, his mind frantic, his mouth dry. He thought of trying to get on the buffalo's back, but that seemed improbable. The buffalo saved him the decision.

With a mighty toss of its head, Malone was thrown up and over, landing face first in a smear of dung. He scrambled to his feet, turning his head in time to see the buffalo whirl and charge after him, head lowered.

Now the entire herd was running, Malone in their midst, trying to tear the buffalo hide from his body. He tripped on the hide, went down, and rose again, running for the edge of the herd, the buffalo on his heels.

Finally he stripped the buffalo hide from his shoulders and lunged clear of the trampling herd. He ran an all-out sprint for the knoll, where his horse stood calmly observing all of this, then stopped, realizing that the bull buffalo was no longer behind him.

The big animal was mauling the hide Malone had cast off, goring it and trampling it into the mud, shaking its massive head with a vengeance.

Malone sagged to the earth, his arms around his knees, taking deep, painful breaths as the bull stamped the battered hide into the mud and finally, tossing its head with a triumphant snort, ambled off to rejoin the scattered herd.

Holzer—without his shaggy, ridiculous robe—Schotte, and the woman were rushing to where he sat, taking in deep, cold breaths, the sweat trickling down his shirt front. Schotte was the first to reach Malone.

"Damn it," the doctor exploded, "you've ruined the morning's work! I told you not to let them run!"

Malone thought of a hundred easy answers. He stared at the man, not believing it. He did the hard thing—he made no reply. Malone only shook his head wearily and lay back against the grass, the coming sun warm on his bruised body, and closed his eyes, shutting out Dr. Schotte and all his nasty humpies.

seven ━━━━━━━━━━━━━━━

Warner Conway had occasion to wear his dress blues that morning. It wasn't required, but it seemed a small gesture, a token of respect.

The services were held after roll call. Neither Mc-Cormack nor Benchley had folks back East, so they were buried outside the sod walls of Outpost Nine, Warner Conway reading from the Good Book over the two flag-draped coffins, which still smelled of pine resin.

Catha Haversham was there, silent, head bowed, but what her thoughts were, Conway could not have guessed. He hoped that this service for two men killed while fighting hostiles might bring home to the Cherokee woman much of what he had been saying to her.

When he was finished, Conway closed the Bible and led the slow walk back into the outpost. A few friends of the dead men lingered for a time; others turned away quickly, not liking the specter of death so near.

Reb McBride had blown taps over the graves, and now he turned, his bugle tucked under his arm. Glancing to the south, he saw the incoming riders, squinted into the sun, and finally identified Malone and Wolfgang Holzer and the two civilians.

McBride made his way back to the barracks, reaching

it on foot about the time Malone did on horseback. Malone swung down, and as he did, he carried with him a stench of dung and brackish water. His uniform was sodden, his face scratched, and he moved stiffly. McBride started to ask what had happened, but the glower on Malone's face was enough to fend him off.

Holzer looked much better, and happier. He jumped down from his horse—actually a one-legged hop—and waved to McBride. He shouted something about "diligent humpies" and then led his horse and Malone's toward the paddock, where a patrol under Fitzgerald was forming up.

Holzer walked past Fitzgerald and Taylor, snapped a salute, which took both junior officers by surprise, and unsaddled his horses, rubbing them down thoroughly before turning them loose in the paddock.

"That's the happiest man on this post," Fitzgerald said, nodding in wonder at Holzer.

"You've obviously never seen his partner with a pint of whiskey in him," Taylor answered with a grin. That gave him pause to consider—where was Malone? He should have taken care of his own horse, not handed that task over to Holzer.

"Where's Malone, Holzer?" Taylor called. "Is he all right?"

Holzer walked all the way across the paddock, saluted again, and clicked his heels together. "Too diligent, sir," Holzer told the officer.

Taylor knew he wouldn't get anything much more comprehensible out of Private Holzer, so he shrugged and dismissed the man with a snappy salute. Holzer returned the salute, clicked his heels again—in imitation of a Prussian uncle, someone had said—and did a neat about-face.

"That man should be a corporal," Fitzgerald said, watching Holzer go.

"He would be, I imagine, if..." Taylor sentence dangled unfinished. The *if* was a big one. Most corporals in the United States Army could speak and understand English. Most.

"He's certainly—" Fitzgerald groped for a word and Taylor supplied it.

"Diligent."

Taylor saw to his horse, but his thoughts were elsewhere. Matt Kincaid had gone this morning; he would actually be in Denver in three days. Taylor's thought drifted irresistibly to the Otard-Dupuy, and he sighed.

Fitzgerald was mounted, watching him curiously, and so Taylor stepped into the stirrup himself. This was one of the new "visibility" patrols Captain Conway had decided upon. There was no target, no idea that a hostile would even be sighted, let alone engaged.

They were simply to make a loop of the southwest quadrant, showing themselves to any Indians out there who might be dreaming up something.

Haversham was being briefed this morning, and this afternoon, when Fitz and Taylor returned, they were going to ride out to the agency to show the shavetail some real Indians.

Taylor was daydreaming. This was going to be a boring morning and a boring afternoon tacked onto the tail end of a thousand identical, lifeless days. Fitzgerald was watching him closely.

"What's the matter?"

"Nothing. This is really a yawn, though, isn't it?"

"It is. Captain thinks it's necessary. Would you rather do some OD time?"

"Walk around rattling doors?" Taylor laughed. "No, I'd rather be where Matt is." He gazed southward, though the coach was long gone.

"We'll think of something to liven this up."

"You have something in mind?" Taylor asked.

"Not yet," Fitzgerald answered. His smile was devious, and he told Taylor in a lowered voice, "But, God, Taylor, we got us a green shavetail. I'm not going to pass up the chance to jab him a little."

"Initiate the man?"

"That's it. He's so green he creaks. Never been West—

besides, think of what Haversham is up to every night while we're staring at the ceiling."

Taylor did think of Catha Haversham, in more detail than was proper. "I see what you mean. That does stir up a man's resentment."

"Among other things," Fitzgerald said. "We've got to cook up something. The man deserves no mercy."

"And I thought you were above petty jealousy," Taylor said. Fitzgerald only tugged his hat down a little, shading his eyes, then turned and nodded to Corporal Wojensky, who swung the patrol to follow the two scheming officers out of Number Nine and onto the broad, sun-dried plains.

There was only one man in the patrol who was not bored stiff. The officers knew this was a routine patrol, more an exercise for the horses than anything else, and that feeling, if not the certain knowledge of this, had sifted down through the ranks. Only Duckworth rode straight in the saddle, eyes squinting into the sun, constantly searching the horizon.

This was his first experience on the plains, his first patrol with Easy Company, and he rode with a certain excitement rising within him. It was good to be on a strong horse among solid men who knew their business. Duckworth tried not to let his thoughts wander to his unspoken fears.

He knew he was not tough, not in the sense that Malone and Dillson were tough, but he was deathly afraid that he might be a coward. How in God's name was a man to know until the time came? He did not want to let Easy Company down, to freeze as he had heard of some men doing—to panic, as others had done, and turn tail. Yet how was a man to know?

Something hard jabbed him roughly in the thigh, bringing Duckworth out of his morbid reveries. He glanced at the man who rode beside him. But Dillson's bulldog face was angelic. Duckworth rubbed his leg and turned his eyes to the front. His leg was jabbed again, harder yet, and Duckworth caught what was happening.

Dillson was swiveling his Springfield, which rode beneath his saddle on that contraption they called a "spider," and jamming it into Duckworth's leg.

They were the last two men in the column, and no one else was aware of Dillson's little game. Duckworth kept his eyes forward, trying to ignore it, but Dillson did it again, jamming the rifle barrel against Duckworth's already bruised leg.

"Dammit, Dillson!"

"What's the matter baby boy?" Dillson asked in an insufferably mocking tone. "Is baby boy mad?"

"You know what's the matter. Knock it off."

Duckworth eased his horse a little to one side, but Dillson followed and again poked his thigh with the Springfield.

"What's the matter, half-pint? Getting salty with old Dillson, are you? Sorry Private Malone ain't here to take care of his baby boy?"

Rafferty was ahead of them, and his head turned back to see what was happening, but there was nothing Rafferty or any of them could do to protect Duckworth from this stupid bullying. The little man would have to stand on his own feet like the rest of them.

Dillson prodded Duckworth again, with savage maliciousness. The pain went through the thigh muscle and into the bone, it seemed.

"I'm warning you!" Duckworth said, but this only encouraged Dillson, who repeated his attack time and again. At intervals he left off, and then, when Duckworth had grown easy about it, a sudden jab of pain brought back his torment.

There was nothing to do about it that Duckworth could see. He could only drift so far away from Dillson and remain in the column. He couldn't shoot the man—although he damned well felt like it—and he couldn't start shouting.

At Dirty Tanks they would water the horses, he thought reassuringly. Then, when they formed up again, no matter what, he would not ride beside Dillson. They were together now, in the rear where all the dust was, only because they were both new men and no one wanted to ride beside the big man. Somehow, Duckworth vowed, he would switch places. A jab in the leg brought Duckworth's head around violently. His face was crimson, the tears in his eyes from anger as well as pain, but that damned Dillson was just grinning, grinning, daring the little man to try something.

Duckworth shut his eyes against the pain and looked forward, hoping for his first glimpse of Dirty Tanks.

Fitzgerald dabbed the sweat from his throat with his scarf, turned to glance back at the column, and mopped his throat again. In spite of the bitterly-cold nights they had been having lately, the days were furnace-hot. A man spent half his time peeling off clothes and putting them back on. He wiped the sweat from his eyes and started to tuck his kerchief away. It was then that the idea came to him, and he smiled slowly. It wasn't a nice smile, but then it was born of an evil idea.

"I've got it," he said to Taylor.

Taylor, whose thoughts had been a thousand miles and a case of Otard-Dupuy away, was slow in responding.

"What?"

"I've got it. A nice surprise for Mr. Haversham."

"Suitably nasty, I trust."

The smile on Fitzgerald's face broadened. "Tell me what you think."

They discussed it as they rode on toward Dirty Tanks, and with the telling, Taylor began to smile too. It was a lousy thing to do to a new man—and just the ticket.

Duckworth glanced at the two lieutenants as they drew up to the water hole. They both seemed to be in amazingly good spirits. Duckworth wished he could say the same, but his leg was throbbing with pain. When he dismounted, he found that his leg was stiffening on him. He would have liked to drop his pants to see what his thigh looked like, but he saw Dillson grinning evilly at him, and he decided not to give the man the satisfaction.

Duckworth had no choice but to ride beside Dillson all

the way back to the outpost, but he had managed to form up on the opposite side, away from the menacing rifle. He had only to endure the stream of verbal abuse that Dillson heaped on him, apparently finding that every bit as entertaining as the prodding.

The gates of Outpost Number Nine were a welcome sight. The flag fluttered uncertainly in the light, sporadic breeze. Duckworth saw to his horse and walked stiffly back to the barracks. Malone was there, and he watched with dark curiosity as Duckworth dropped his trousers to reveal a purplish-yellow bruise extending over nearly his entire thigh.

"What happened?" Malone asked.

"None of your damned business," Duckworth snapped. He didn't need a bodyguard.

"Pardon me," Malone said, drawling sarcastically. He leaned back in his bunk, closing his eyes but not sleeping.

It wasn't until dinner that Rafferty told Malone what Dillson had done to the little man. "The son of a bitch is out-and-out vicious, Malone. He was hitting on Duckworth because you backed him down the other day. That's why Ducks wouldn't tell you about it, I guess. It's a little like running to Daddy."

"It'll happen anyway," Malone said over his last cup of coffee. "Me and Dillson, I mean. He'll rile me once too often."

"I wouldn't mess with him," Rafferty said soberly.

"Think I can't handle him?"

"I don't know. Maybe so. But he'll come back on you. He's plain mean and sneaky." Then Rafferty told Malone what had happened with Dillson and Lieutenant Fitzgerald.

Malone pondered it silently, his eyes sullen. "Think he would have done it? Think it was Fitzgerald he was really after?"

"I don't know. Only Dillson knows for sure, I guess. Maybe Wraps-Up-His-Tail just happened to pop into his sights and he killed him out of instinct. I'll tell you though, Reb was there, and he's damned sure it was Fitz that Dillson wanted to kill."

"No way of proving it," Malone shrugged.

"No way. That's why none of us has said anything. There'd be a big investigation, proving nothing. You can't read a man's mind."

Malone was silent for a long minute, turning his cup in his hands. He looked around and then said in a lowered voice to Rafferty, "Maybe something ought to be done about Private Dillson. You know, there's others besides Fitzgerald that could be accidentally shot."

"That's not your style, Malone."

"No." He shook his head in agreement. "But if it gets to the point where it looks like it's him or one of us—it just might get to be my style."

The thought of what could only be labeled murder turned Rafferty's stomach, yet there was some logic to Malone's line of reasoning. Dillson would kill somebody, given time, as that hatred of his fermented. Malone said no more about it, nor did Rafferty, but the idea had lodged in their minds and they carried it with them back to the barracks.

Fitzgerald and Taylor's plan was less brutal, but more clearly formulated. They began working on Haversham the moment the three junior officers had cleared the front gate.

"How far to the Indian agency?" Haversham asked.

"An hour," Taylor said. He glanced at Fitzgerald, and Fitz began it.

"It's quite important to understand these people, Everett. I mean to understand what makes them tick."

"Oh, I agree," Haversham said, taking the bait eagerly. "It's one reason I'm anxious to visit the agency Cheyenne."

"But it's a shame..." Fitzgerald fell silent. He stretched out a hand and flicked a deerfly from his horse's ear.

"What were you saying?" Haversham asked.

"Oh, just that it's a shame that the Cheyenne are so reticent. I mean it really takes years to get inside their thoughts."

"Well, their entire culture is different."

"Certainly. If one hasn't been accepted..." Fitzgerald's voice faded away again, and he shrugged.

"Do I understand you to mean that some whites are taken into their confidence?" Haversham inquired.

"Well, of course," Fitzgerald answered. "Those who have been initiated into the tribe."

Neither Fitzgerald nor Taylor would add any more, although they had Haversham's curiosity aroused. He felt they were holding back something from him. They dipped into a long, sandy wash and climbed the far bank, chasing a coyote from the wash. It loped off, a dead jackrabbit in its jaws, its tail curled between its legs.

"You know how eager I am to get inside the Cheyenne mind," Haversham said. "I mean for Catha's sake as well as my own."

Neither man answered him.

"If there was a way, that is."

"You wouldn't want to try it," Taylor said offhandedly.

"Is there a way?" He looked from one man to the other. Receiving no answer, he went on, "Is it that the initiation would be dangerous? I mean, I've heard tales of these Sun Dances and all."

"Oh, it's nothing like that," Taylor assured him. "But uncomfortable, I suppose. Besides, there's not a chance in a hundred that Slow Bird would accept you."

"No?"

"I could talk to him," Fitzgerald said. Then he waved a hand as if that were a bad idea. "No. Very little chance."

"We could ask."

"He'd never consent."

"You know, Fitz, we could mention that Haversham's wife is Cherokee."

"Would that swing any weight?"

"Doubtful, but it might."

Haversham was totally intrigued now. His face was anxiously insistent. "You really must try, Fitz. What exactly is involved—I mean, you do know, don't you?"

"Not entirely. Taylor and I were refused."

"It's a purification rite," Taylor explained. "Some sort of steambath on the surface, but the rite has a great significance symbolically."

"But I mean, if you two were refused—" Haversham said dismally.

His hopes had been rising. To be able to return to the outpost and inform Catha that he had actually been initiated into the Cheyenne brotherhood! That should prove something to her—that her ideas were not so farfetched—if he, a white, could become a brother to the Cheyenne, understand them, be one of them. On a purely practical level, it seemed that a man who knew the Cheyenne more intimately might be better able to cope with them in terms of both peace and friendship.

Taylor had been silent, but now he added a clincher, "If what they say about that ritual is true, it might be dangerous." Fitzgerald agreed with a nod of the head.

"In what way?" Haversham asked.

"Well, it's that it is supposed to make a man utterly virile—if you get my meaning. Of course, your case is different from ours. Maybe to you . . . is your spring wound well enough, Haversham?"

"Is my—?" Haversham suddenly got Taylor's meaning. There had been times lately . . . after all, Catha was a robust woman. "Is that the dangerous side effect you're talking about?"

"Dangerous to a lone man out here," Taylor replied. "Wouldn't you say? I mean, I can't see myself trying to sneak up on a buffalo cow."

"I see what you mean," Haversham said thoughtfully. "Of course, I. . . ." He let the delicate subject drop.

They rode in silence for a mile after that, the breeze flattening the long grass before them. A lone crow, high in the crystal sky, wheeled and cawed against the day.

Haversham was hooked, they knew it. Fitzgerald spared a covert grin for Taylor. He wasn't sure which point of the two-pronged attack had gotten to Haversham, but he was hooked good. Fitzgerald could read it in his face, particularly in his eyes, which shone with anticipation.

Fitzgerald began again, expressing doubt that the medicine man, Slow Bird, would ever consent to this initiation. That only served to whet Haversham's desire. By the time

91

they reached the agency he was jittery with eagerness.

Haversham was hardly impressed by his first Cheyenne Indians. Lethargically he toured the beef pens, the agency store, the feeble garden, which was overgrown with weeds and parched to the point of no return.

"What's the matter, Everett?" Fitzgerald asked. They stood in the shade of a lightning-struck oak, mopping their faces, passing a canteen.

"Nothing's the matter. It's just that I had hoped—this medicine man, Slow Bird, I thought we were going to speak with him."

"Oh, well, maybe later. You've spoken to some others."

"For all the good it did me," Haversham said with some annoyance.

"Well"—Fitzgerald shrugged—"you're an outsider, as we warned you." He didn't mention the fact that most of the Cheyenne they had tried to speak with had as much English as Haversham had Bulgarian.

"That's what I mean," Haversham said with quiet exasperation. "I really want to know these people."

"The initiation again," Taylor said, shaking his head.

"That's right."

None of them mentioned the second alleged effect of the Cheyenne sweat lodge, but it lingered in the rear of Haversham's mind. Two sure methods to suitably impress Catha were represented by that Cheyenne sweat lodge. From where they now stood, Haversham could even see it: a squat, dome-shaped structure made of hides on bent willow poles.

There could hardly be a more unimposing structure on all of the plains, but to Haversham just then, it seemed to glow with golden promise.

"There he is," Fitzgerald said at his elbow. Haversham glanced to the right, where an old, hunched Indian wearing a white blanket, his hair tied in a single braid, walked slowly through the sage toward the sweat lodge.

"Is that Slow Bird?" Haversham asked. His voice was nearly reverent.

"None other."

"Talk to him," Haversham said quickly.

"It won't do any good."

"You've got to give it a try."

"I'll try," Fitzgerald said, "but I'll have the devil's own time trying to convince him."

He gripped Haversham's arm tightly, and then strode off to meet the medicine man, who glanced up with surprise. The convincing was a lot easier than Fitzgerald had told Haversham. It took exactly one silver dollar to persuade Slow Bird to agree to let the white soldier torture himself.

Fitzgerald dragged it out as long as possible. He waved his arms and shook his head. From the shade where Haversham waited, it looked like Fitzgerald was pleading, cajoling, arguing on his behalf.

To Slow Bird, who had already agreed and now stood there, dollar in hand, watching the crazy soldier wave his arms and harangue him, the entire business was incomprehensible. But then he had always suspected all whites were crazy.

"Wait here," Fitzgerald said. Slow Bird shrugged and watched as Fitzgerald strode purposefully back to Haversham and shook his head mournfully. "He wants to be sure your wife is Indian."

"You know she is."

"I know, but I can't convince him."

"Try lifting your hand," Taylor put in. "You know—the peace sign."

Uncertainly, Haversham lifted his hand, palm toward Slow Bird, who shrugged and lifted his own hand.

"I don't see what—" Haversham began, but Fitzgerald cut him off.

"It's not going to work if you can't prove it," Fitzgerald said worriedly.

"Dammit, I can't!"

"All right." He held Haversham's arm and looked again, with great weariness, at Slow Bird. "I'll try."

Haversham's silent gratitude was overwhelming. He watched as Fitzgerald hiked back toward the waiting Indian, and said to Taylor, "There goes a hell of a man."

"Isn't he, though," Taylor said, hiding his smile behind his hand as he coughed. He needn't have bothered. Everett Haversham's eyes were fixed on Fitzgerald, who was standing before Slow Bird once more, obviously pleading his case with the instincts and passion of a country lawyer. Finally, after an interminable wait, he saw Fitzgerald turn, beckon to them, and stand watching, a triumphant smile on his lips.

"I hope it's worth it, Haversham," Fitzgerald said, still managing a straight face.

"I'm sure it will be." Impulsively, Haversham took Fitzgerald's hand. "I won't forget this," he promised.

A puzzled Slow Bird led Haversham off toward the sweat house, and Taylor, watching them go, said, "I'll bet you won't."

Slow Bird guided Haversham to the entrance of the sweat lodge. He made motions to indicate that Haversham should strip, and the man did so, standing naked before the Cheyenne.

The old man was sober and ritualistic in his movements, carefully stoking the fire, which was built over stones set in a symbolic pattern. As the fire took hold, Slow Bird went outside and placed buffalo hides over the openings that served as windows. One space was left open—the door where Haversham had entered the hut.

Slow Bird spoke in English, surprising Haversham. "The sun breeds life." His hand waved skyward. "In its passing, the life is given to the earth. Goodness. Yet many men do not know how to recover this goodness. It has hidden in the wild things, in the stones, the trees."

As he spoke, he also stripped, then squatted and arranged a dozen narrow sticks before him in a pattern that was meaningless to Haversham. The old Cheyenne glanced up with dark eyes sunken deeply into a weather-lined face.

He continued with his instruction. "When there is steam, the good vapors can rise from the stone." His hand lifted again, his fingers wriggling in an imitation of rising smoke.

94

"The goodness meets the body, meets the mind of a man—the soul, that is. The bad spirits in the body are forced to flee. They ooze from the skin and are overcome by the steam. And so a man is purified."

He looked expectantly at Haversham, but Everett had no response to make. He simply stood there, feeling himself in the presence of a mystical truth.

The medicine man motioned to Haversham, indicating that he should squat by the fire as he himself was doing. Then the last skins were lowered and the room became dark, the heat intense.

A sound like a pistol shot startled Haversham, and then he realized that the medicine man had taken a mouthful of water from a gourd dipper and spit a stream of water onto the fire-heated stones.

Haversham was squatting on his heels, but still his head scraped the low roof of the medicine hut. His hair was so hot now, as the steam rose and curled around him, that he could hardly touch it. He became concerned that it would singe off. But apparently the concern was foolish, since Slow Bird still had his full head of hair.

Haversham closed his eyes, concentrating on the steam, which was not utterly oppressive. He became dazed and dizzy with the heat. Sweat poured off his body, stinging his eyes. Slow Bird passed him the gourd dipper, and he poured the water gratefully over his head. It seemed to clear his brain with a hot mist, bringing a rush of colors. Brilliant yellow and crimson. He had a sharp, compelling image of a horseman riding naked across the vast purple plains. He blinked, but that changed nothing. The heat, which had nearly overcome him, seemed to recede as he concentrated on the image in his mind.

The horseman seemed to be Haversham himself, and at the same time to be a Cheyenne warrior in full battle regalia. He sat on a low ridge, where a cool breeze swept up from the deep gorge below. An eagle soared past and was struck by a golden arrow.

Alone, now standing in the deep grass, Haversham saw

the eagle plunge to its death. He turned, and tears of steam ran from his eyes, but the woman was rushing toward him. Catha—or was it a Cheyenne maiden?—naked and alive, long hair flowing down her back as her lithe body rushed into his embrace.

The sweat rained down Haversham's body. The smile on his face was unmistakable. But it was over. Suddenly there was light and fresh air. Slow Bird, his blanket around his narrow shoulders, stood silently watching Haversham.

Then the medicine man gave a satisfied grunt and walked from the sweat lodge. Haversham did not move for a long moment. The fresh breeze swept the steam away, and with it the vision—he didn't know what else to call it.

Unsteadily he rose and dressed and, utterly satisfied, walked out to where Taylor and Fitzgerald lay against the grass, watching him.

"I'll never be able to thank you enough," Haversham said. The two men rose, exchanging puzzled glances, and Haversham solemnly took their hands.

"It was...all right?" Taylor asked in disbelief.

"It was revealing, beautiful. The eagle. The woman on the plains." His face positively glowed.

Fitzgerald asked, "It was enjoyable? I mean, all that heat!"

"The heat passed away like a dream," Haversham said distantly. His eyes were focused on a far distant point. He added with a faint smile, "And I have the strongest urge to be with my wife. Thank you. Thank you."

He sat on the grass, crosslegged, and became lost in his own thoughts. Fitzgerald moved away a little, Taylor on his heels.

"Hell of a joke. The man acts like he's just had a quick trip to paradise."

"What do you think happened?" Taylor asked, still looking at Haversham. "What did he see?"

"It makes a man wonder," Fitzgerald admitted.

"I can't get over it. Do you suppose we've been missing out on something all this time?"

"No," Fitzgerald said disparagingly. "Still...see if you can catch Slow Bird. Hell, it can't hurt to try it."

"He doesn't look hurt, that's for damned sure."

Taylor was already moving, even as he talked. Slow Bird was near the stream, filling his water jug, and after a moment's conversation, two dollars passed between them. Haversham glanced up dreamily a minute later to see the Cheyenne leading Fitzgerald and Taylor to the sweat lodge, and he lifted a hand to them. They waved back and then were ushered inside the sweat lodge. Haversham lay back, shutting his eyes in contemplation.

He dozed. The sun was warm on his face, the dry grass a comfortable cushion. He doubted that he had ever felt better in his life.

Fitzgerald *knew* he had felt better. He wasn't sure whether he had ever felt worse. The sweat poured out of him, and his mind was awash with dizzy confusion. He squatted there naked in the steam-obscured interior of the hut, which stank of green hides, feeling as if his skin were aflame. He glanced at Taylor, who was, if anything, more uncomfortable.

The sweltering heat had sledgehammered Taylor into hopeless immobility. He simply endured it as a man endures pain and illness, hoping against hope that the torment will end. But Slow Bird spat more water against the stones and the steam rose up again, curling into red ears, watery eyes, dry mouth and lungs. Taylor closed his eyes and his head started to drum again, his legs to tremble, and silently, fluently he cursed Mr. Haversham.

When it had ended, they staggered into the clear light of day on rubbery legs, their flesh chilled by the sudden wave of cool wind that had risen with the sinking of the sun. They dressed with their teeth chattering, their muscles hopelessly rubberlike, then stood together glaring at the hillside where Haversham sat contentedly, a blade of grass between his lips.

"He suckered us, Fitz. Damned if he didn't. What an actor."

"He did, didn't he? Turned it right around on us. By God—" He regarded Taylor, who was limp, dehydrated, and dismal-looking, and Fitzgerald suddenly burst out laughing. Taylor watched him somberly, and after a while his mouth formed into a sympathetic smile.

"Just don't let on that it got to us," Fitzgerald cautioned him. "Maybe we didn't stick him, but don't give him the satisfaction of knowing he got us. Ready?" Fitzgerald straightened his tunic and put on a brave smile. "Let's go on up there now. Swagger a little, man, good."

Haversham watched them returning, saw the smiles on their faces, and felt good about the day. "All of us," he said, putting a hand on each man's shoulder. "Brothers now." Seriously he added, "What you did for me—I can never repay it."

"We've been repaid," Taylor muttered. Haversham glanced at him, but said nothing.

"It'll be dark before we get back if we don't ride," Fitzgerald said quickly. They rode silently back to Outpost Number Nine, and Fitzgerald kicked himself mentally all the way. *Practical jokes*, he thought with a shudder. But damn, that Haversham was good. He glanced over and saw that Everett Haversham was still grinning, his eyes still bright, and in disgust Fitzgerald heeled his surprised horse into a long run across the prairie.

Catha had an entirely different reaction. She was surprised and thrilled that Everett had taken this initial step toward finding brotherhood with the Cheyenne.

"If only," she told him, "I could have been there. It makes me feel so hopeful about the rest of my plans."

"Those plans. You can't still be holding onto them, Catha."

"And why not?" she asked with a pert toss of her head.

"After what Captain Conway and the others have said to you?"

"What have they said? That there is a battle going on here?"

"Yes, a battle. You know blood is being spilled out there. You saw the dead soldiers."

"I know, Everett," she said with a conciliatory smile, "But there is a difference between an armed soldier in uniform and an unarmed Indian woman."

"Perhaps not to the Cheyenne."

"To anyone, Everett."

He was slowly undressing, and she watched him for a minute, taking in the narrow waist, the broad, flat chest of her husband, all so familiar, yet still so new to her.

"I can't cast aside my ideas so easily, Everett. They are my brothers and sisters—those strange people of the Plains. I can hardly stop caring about them because someone recommends it. Any more than I could stop loving you on command."

He was seated on the cane chair now, completely naked exhibiting an obvious, rising interest in Catha, who wordlessly began to unfasten her calico dress after first unpinning her luxuriant dark hair.

"Anyway, we had better talk about it," Everett said.

She slipped from her dress, standing before him proudly, her flesh golden in the lantern light, her dark nipples taut and eager. His eyes swept over her, to linger at the apex of her smooth, tapered thighs, where her soft, dark patch of hair flourished.

"Did the steambath really make you feel...excited?" Catha asked her husband. She moved toward him, but her movement was slow, calculated to give him time to enjoy her tantalizing body. She knew that he enjoyed looking upon her, taking in the nuances of shadow and light, curve and angle, swell and taper of her perfect figure.

Looking at him, she could see how eager he was now. His erection rose between his legs as he sat rigidly in the cane chair, his eyes glazed.

"What?" he murmured.

"Did the steam bath advance your virility?" she asked with a teasing smile.

"I'd like to find out."

99

"And so would I. Although what you could have gained, I don't know. You already have more than enough."

"Too much?"

"Never too much, Everett." She stood so near to him that their knees brushed.

"At times I do get tired," he admitted.

"I too. I exhaust myself against you, Everett, wanting to pummel you, devour you." She slid onto his lap, facing him, her legs straddling his, and he felt the damp touch of her against his thigh. She leaned forward, threw her arms around his neck, and kissed him.

"You're a nice man, apart from the fact that I'm madly in love with you, Mr. Haversham."

"You're so beautiful, Catha." He was intoxicated with her beauty. He had begun trembling, all the way down to his feet, and his erection wavered and sought her like a cobra rising between his legs.

She pressed forward and he felt the warm contact of her breasts against his chest, felt her lift herself slightly and, with a deeply contented smile, settle onto him. Haversham felt the shuddering focus itself in his erection. It twitched spasmodically within Catha, and she felt it. Smiling, she leaned more tightly against him, her strong arms holding him with all her might.

"This other business, Catha," Haversham said as he nuzzled her shoulder, kissing her through the screen of her fine dark hair, "we'll have to talk about it."

"Yes," she murmured. She kissed his ear, and it was like touching a flame to it. He felt her hips rise, felt the sweetly insistent tugging of her body. "We'll speak about it all, Everett. Later," she said softly. "Later, dear Everett."

And he agreed.

eight ————————————

It was freezing cold. The rising half moon silhouetted the silent guards tramping back and forth along the parapet. Malone leaned sleepily against a porch upright, arms crossed, head bowed, legs crossed at the ankles. Wolfgang Holzer walked back and forth, vigorously slapping his shoulders, trying to keep warm. In the distance a coyote howled, and a dog in the Indian camp across the deadline picked up the howl.

Schotte came briskly out of his quarters, carrying his heavy packs, which he strapped onto the patiently waiting mules. Clara Marlowe peered nervously out the door, disappeared momentarily, and reappeared minutes later, canteens slung over her narrow shoulder. She turned out the lamp beside the door and stepped out into the chill morning.

"Good morning, Private Malone."

"Mornin', ma'am. Off to try it again, are we?"

"Until this area is done," she said with a quick nod of her head. "Although I understand we're being restricted from traveling farther west just now. Has there been Indian trouble?"

"Now and again," Malone answered. "Then you'll be through with this foolishness?"

"Foolishness!" Her anger was made ridiculous by her reed-thin voice and small stature, and Malone grinned. "It's hardly foolish, Private Malone."

"Looked mighty foolish to me yesterday," he told her.

"Only because you bungled it," she said tartly.

"Oh." He nodded seriously. "Is that it?"

Then he looked at her and grinned again. It infuriated her and she stamped away on tiny feet, struggling to lift her saddle. Two strong arms encircled her and she gasped.

But it was only the saddle Malone was interested in. He hefted it as she ducked under his arm and stood aside, her hand raised protectively to her throat.

Malone smoothed her saddle blanket and tossed the saddle over the gray's back. He noticed it was a Texas rig—double-cinched, with a high cantle.

"Nice saddle. Kind I favor. The army, unfortunately, favors McClellans."

"A soldier in Colorado gave it to me. We'd lost ours on the train. He said the same thing—he liked it, but there was little point in keeping it. The army is fussy about regimentation, it seems."

"It can be."

"You've been a cowboy, Private Malone?"

"Some."

"But no longer."

"No."

He held the bridle while she mounted. He thought of his cowboying briefly. It hadn't been a long career, but in retrospect it seemed it had been a good life. He had damn sure made decent money—a dollar a day, compared to the thirteen a month he made soldiering.

But, by God, he had gotten tired of those nights out, the flash floods, the stampedes, looking at the butt end of a thousand cows . . . he smiled to himself, thinking it was just about what he was doing this week, herding those buffalo. But in Texas they let you use a horse for that kind of work. It saved the boots.

They rode silently through the gate, which creaked on its massive hinges. The plains were frosted, silver under the silver moon, the trees huddled in dark groups along the bottoms.

Malone found himself beside Clara Marlowe, and she didn't look like she felt much like talking, but Malone did.

"Hell of a time you've had for yourself, ain't it? Traipsing all around for eighteen months, counting these damned buffalo?"

"Wearying," she admitted. "But fun in a way. Some of my associates in Washington promised me I'd see as much of the West as anyone since Lewis and Clark, traveling with Dr. Schotte, and they were right."

"Hell of a dry old bird, ain't he?"

"Dr. Schotte!" Her voice was both questioning and defensive. "Maybe just a little," she confided.

"Hell of a job. I need a job I can understand," Malone said.

"You mean a simple job?" she suggested, and he laughed.

"Maybe so."

They were silent for a time, watching the dark, silent plains. Malone tried to explain what he had meant. "You see, with cattle you've got five hundred in the herd. Maybe you drive 'em three hundred miles. You see two fall by the wayside, watch the Indians cut out five. You know you've got four hundred and—"

"Ninety-three," Clara prompted.

"Four hundred ninety-three cows. But you take these buffalo. You count a hundred. Six get shot by Indians, twenty by some buffalo hunters, wolves take two. The rain washes the damned whitewash off their butts. How many you got left? No tellin', because you don't even know how many you had to start with."

"And so the project makes no sense to you?"

"That's about it, ma'am."

"It is difficult, and of course whatever we determine to be the actual number can only be a rough estimate," she agreed, "but it will be more than we had before."

"And so what?" Malone said. "Who's it matter to?"

"It should matter to everyone," she said a little heatedly. "They are a natural resource. There's a lot of meat on a buffalo. It matters, Private Malone, believe me. Especially to the Indian. Did you ever consider how much a part of their life it is?"

"You mean like eating buffalo, wearing its hide and all?"

"And all is exactly what I mean, Private Malone. Besides eating the meat, making his home from the buffalo hides, the Indian uses hides, horns, hoofs, and innards—and dung for fire, as you know. Every bit of that buffalo is used for all manner of things."

"Moccasins and all, you mean?"

"And all," she sighed with thinly veiled impatience. "From the bone, hide-scrapers can be made. Knives, sewing awls, arrowheads, dice, hoes—"

"Hold it, hold it!" Malone laughed, but Clara had caught fire.

"From the hides they make tipis, bedcovers, medicine cases, caps, leggings, dresses, saddle covers, saddlebags, bridles, hobbles, travois hitches, watering troughs!"

"Ma'am," Malone said, "I didn't mean—" But she went on, counting the items on her fingers even after she had run out of fingers.

"From buffalo horns, powder flasks are made, spoons, cups, honda rings—"

"Miss Marlowe—"

"Skins are tanned with boiled residue of brains, fat, and liver. Bowstrings are made from sinews, thread from the same material. Why, Private Malone, they even make rattles out of dried buffalo scrotums."

"Out of what, ma'am?"

"Scrotums," she said in a quieter voice. Her enthusiasm had tapered off into acute embarrassment.

"I'm afraid I don't know what that word means, Miss Marlowe. Just what is that now?"

"Well," she stuttered, "the buffalo—I mean the male buffalo—has a . . . sack, you see."

"When you skin him out?" Malone asked. His face was in the shadow of the hat, and Clara could not see his expression. His voice seemed simply curious.

"No. It's not an internal organ, Private Marlowe. External."

"Oh." Malone was thoughtful. "*Ex*ternal."

"Yes."

"I don't get it. Now, ma'am," he asked, turning in his saddle, "is it only buffalo now that has these whatchacallems?"

"Scrotums, no," she muttered, turning her eyes away.

"Now that sure is a new one on me." Malone rubbed his jaw. "Is there any other name I might know these scrowtums by?"

"I don't... none that I can think of," she said hastily. Her face was hot, and she knew she was flushed to a deep red, which the night concealed from Malone.

"That surely is a new one on me. Scrow-tums, huh? Well, well."

They continued in silence, which Clara found welcome. Now a line of gold appeared in the east, brilliantly edging the low hills. Minutes later the skies flushed red with the coming of dawn, and Schotte, turning his head, called to Clara. She rode to join him, greatly relieved, while Malone, grinning, slapped his horse's neck and eased over to ride silently beside Wolfgang Holzer.

The area where they would work this morning was low ground. Much of it was boggy and overgrown with cattails and reeds. An unlikely spot for the bison, but there they were, scattered among the head-high reeds, not gathered up tight as Malone would have expected. Whatever else Schotte was, Malone had to admit he was damned good at finding buffalo. From a half-mile off you couldn't have told anything alive was down among the cattails.

"We won't be able to go at this the same way," Doctor Schotte said.

"Good," Malone put in, but Schotte ignored him.

"We'll split into two parties. I will take Holzer," he said in a way that made it obvious he preferred the German private to Malone; it was also a sort of apology to Clara for leaving her with the likes of Private Malone. "We have to have one experienced observer in each group," he told Clara, again apologetically.

"This will be a rough count?" she asked.

Schotte looked the terrain over. A horseshoe-shaped slough, which obviously became a pond when it rained, circled a flat, broad knoll. "Yes," he sighed. "You'll know how to approach it. Holzer and I will take the south side."

Leaving Malone with Clara, the doctor and Holzer hiked up a game trail along the southern face of the knoll. Schotte glanced back worriedly once, but Clara waved him on.

"Trusts me, doesn't he?" Malone commented.

"You got off on the wrong foot, that's all."

"I do have a way of doing that," he admitted.

The coming sun was warm, so Malone removed his great coat. Clara did the same, leaving behind her fur-lined hat as well. Her mouse-colored hair glinted in the new sunlight, errant strands curling across her forehead, and down her neck. She turned to him, the sunlight flashing on the lenses of her spectacles.

"Ready?"

"I reckon."

"Fine, then on we go. Don't spook them."

There was no equipment to be carried, and fortunately no buffalo hide to wear. She had a pad and pencil in her hand, and that was it. Frail and tiny as she looked, Clara set off at a good pace. By the time they reached the crest of the hummock, Malone was perspiring. He sagged gratefully to the damp, grassy earth as Clara silently indicated they should stop and sit.

Malone, propped up on his elbows, could see only an occasional patch of dark hair below to indicate that any buffalo were actually in the bottoms. Clara, her eyes moving mechanically, in a fixed pattern, searched the slough, her pencil making a tally mark each time she spotted a buffalo.

She was better at it than he would have been, Malone decided. He couldn't make out more than half a dozen among the tall reeds. She had already tallied three times that number in her notebook.

"Miss Marlowe?"

"Sh!"

"That's about all of 'em, ain't it?"

"Shh!" she repeated more forcefully. Malone sighed and looked idly around. It was growing warm, so he stripped off his tunic and undershirt, spreading them on the grass beneath him. He leaned back and closed his eyes, feeling the tingling warmth on his chest.

He half dozed for nearly thirty minutes before he felt the sharp prod of a finger in his ribs. Clara hovered over him.

"We have to get closer," she insisted.

"All right." Lazily, Malone picked up his clothes and followed her down a narrow, gray granite outcropping, through a brush-clotted wash, and onto a second outcropping, where the cattails grew thickly.

Malone had to hold his forearm in front of his face to fend off the prickly cattails. At the very edge of the outcropping, Clara nodded with satisfaction and got to her belly, peering out at the grazing buffalo.

Malone looked around, slapped at a mosquito, and set about trampling down some of the cattails and reeds. Clara turned toward him sharply.

"Sh!"

"Yes, ma'am," he said with a mock salute.

He had his little burrow completed, a six-by-ten patch of flattened reeds, and he spread out his shirt again, lying facedown on the mat of foliage. The scent of the crushed cattails was ripe, pungent, the sun warm on his back. The humming of mosquitoes and the chirping of cicadas soothed Malone, and in a matter of minutes he was peacefully asleep, dreaming briefly of Cora Winchester in that Abilene dance hall.

He awoke sharply, Clara's screams ringing in his ears. Malone pawed his Scoff from its holster and rushed through the reeds, moving in a crouch to the edge of the outcropping, his eyes alert, his first thought of hostiles. He cursed himself for dozing.

Peering over the outcropping, he saw nothing at first—

only a startled buffalo calf, which was attempting to hide by sticking its head into a clump of tall grass, its exposed body quivering with fright.

Then he saw Clara Marlowe and he stood upright, sighed, and tucked his pistol away. She had gotten too close to the edge, apparently, or had tried to clamber down it, for she had fallen into the shoulder-deep wallow at the foot of the outcropping.

"You all right?" he called, cupping his hands to his mouth.

"I can't get out," she said, her voice frantic and embarrassed at the same time.

Only her head and one arm protruded from the wallow, a pond of muddy water and dung, where algae flourished. Her face and hair were slime-covered. Her glasses were lost.

"I'm coming down," he called. "Hold on."

He eased his way down the craggy face of the outcropping, his boots slipping twice, dropping him roughly into a sitting position. The second time, he banged his elbow.

She watched him stoically from the wallow, as if it were quicksand and any movement might pull her inexorably deeper into the mud and slime. Malone had never seen anyone look so downright helpless, beaten, and ashamed.

Reaching the flats, he moved around through the ankle-deep mud to find a stand of willows. With his knife he chopped off a six-foot length of a slender bough and made his way back to where Clara watched patiently through a mask of mud.

Malone sank suddenly to his knees and breathed a curse.

"I can't come any closer," he shouted. "I'll try to pull you out with the pole."

She nodded obediently and Malone stretched out as far as possible. The willow branch fell just short of Clara's straining hand.

Her other hand appeared from under the muck, rising to clutch at the willow, and finally she nodded. Malone braced himself and pulled back. His feet went out from under him and he sat down abruptly in the mud surrounding the wallow.

Grimacing, he stood, wiping his hands on his bare stomach. Bare-chested, mud-spattered, Malone looked completely savage. Clara Marlowe looked like something not of this earth.

He drew her slowly from the incredible suction of the muddy wallow, and she slogged forward, her shirt and skirt heavy with mud, her arms, face, and hair dripping globs of slime.

She stood knee-deep in the mud, simply looking at Malone, as if all the life had been drawn out of her. Always tiny and frail, she now looked like a shadow of a woman, helpless, fragile.

"Think you can climb out of here?" Malone asked, panting.

She looked up the lichen-crusted face of the outcropping and shook her head miserably. Clara Marlowe probably weighed no more than ninety pounds, but she now carried perhaps fifty pounds of mud and mire in her skirts, pockets, petticoats, boots, ears, and hair.

"All right." Malone took three deep breaths before he nodded and said, "I'll try carrying you. Get up on my back now."

He squatted and she climbed onto his back, her legs locking around his hips, her arms throttling him.

"All right," Malone gasped, clutching at her wrists. "You can ease off my throat a little."

"Sorry," she said in a pathetically small voice.

Malone turned his head and looked at her. She was like a child clinging to him, a soaked and sodden little girl who had fallen into a mud puddle and ruined her new clothes.

"All right. Here we go...I hope," he breathed. He started to climb, planting each step cautiously, his fingers searching for handholds. It was thirty feet up, and his back ached with the effort before he had gone halfway. The wind was cold against his back, and his lungs were on fire.

Inching his way up, Malone climbed the lichen-slick

rock, twice misstepping and nearly losing his balance. But he abruptly found the lip of the ledge and crawled onto it, straining shoulders and arms as he rolled up and over, Clara coming free of him to lie flat on her back, her narrow ribcage pounding.

Malone sat beside her, breathing heavily, his arms locked around his knees. His elbow had begun to bleed where he had knocked it and he turned his arm to examine the wound.

"I'm sorry," Clara said, watching him.

"No need to be," he answered. "My fault more'n yours. I should've been watching you."

"I shouldn't need watching," she countered. Her teeth had begun to chatter, and she looked absolutely miserable.

"Well," Malone said, grinning, "I guess we all need some looking after from time to time."

Unaccountably she began to cry. Malone winced—crying women were not his specialty. Her shoulders shuddered and she put her muddy face into her muddy hands and sobbed.

"That's all right," Malone managed to say. Feeling useless, he rose, leaving her to her tears. There had to be a reason she was crying, but it was beyond him. He walked through the reeds to his cubbyhole, found his clean undershirt, and walked back to where Clara Marlowe sat.

"Here," he said, squatting on his haunches. She looked up and he handed her his undershirt.

"I couldn't."

"Do me a favor. Do it," he encouraged her. The mud was starting to dry on her face, becoming a sort of cracked mask.

Clara took the cloth and began wiping her face, her hands. In a few minutes she looked no better, but the shirt was ruined. She held it up and began to bawl again.

"I'm really not like this," she apologized. "I'm sorry."

Malone did his best to smile. They both stank with the algae and the dung. The wind was cool on them. He stretched out a hand, and Clara stared at him.

"What for?" she asked timidly.

110

"We've got to get cleaned up. I'm not going all day like this, are you?"

"How?" She rose to her feet.

"There's a seep, back a ways. Clear water."

"I couldn't."

"Frankly, Miss Marlowe, you smell like a hog. If you won't, I will."

That started the tears again, and Malone looked pleadingly to the skies. "Come on." He took her hand and she followed meekly.

The seep trickled out from between layers of granite, running downhill in a thin, wide sheet to the wallow below. Malone bent to it, rinsing his chest, shoulders, and face as Clara Marlowe watched.

"That's not quite good enough," he told her. "Turn your head if you want." She stared at him uncomprehendingly. Malone unbuckled his belt and she turned away quickly.

He kicked off his boots and dropped his trousers, sitting in the inches-deep water, rubbing the slime from him. Then, still naked, teeth chattering, he washed his trousers as well as possible. Clara still stood within ten feet of him, her mud-caked back hunched, her head unmoving.

"That's it for me. I'm going back to that little hollow to dry out."

She only nodded. Somehow, she herself felt naked. She saw his shadow against the ground from the corner of her eye, and closed her eyes tightly until he was gone. She could see his pale shoulders disappearing through the tall reeds.

Clara turned and watched the seeping water morosely, then she let her clothing drop heavily to the ground.

Malone walked through the brush, the prickly edges of the cattails sharp against his bare flesh. He found his clearing and, hanging up his trousers to dry in the sun, lay down on his clean tunic to let the sun warm him.

He lay on his back, his forearm over his eyes to shield them from the light, and after a while he felt comfortably warm here, out of the wind.

111

He dozed and then came alert, hands clenching. Something had brushed against his ankle, and he lifted his head cautiously.

Clara was there, and it was her hand he had felt on his leg.

"I'm sorry," she said. "I feel so dismal."

"That's all right."

She was naked, her long hair hanging in damp strands. Her flesh was studded with goosebumps. Her breasts, very small but quite firm, stood out from her narrow ribcage. Her eyes, unnaturally large without glasses, peered in his direction. Her hand had never left his ankle.

"I'm sorry. I don't know what's come over me," she said, nervously wagging her head. "I'm all confused . . ." Her face was hesitant, and she seemed unable to order her thoughts, unwilling to think just now. Malone held out a hand.

"It's all right, come here."

She crawled to him and, childlike, curled up against his chest, her knee thrown over his thigh. Malone stroked her damp hair and gently kissed her forehead.

"I'm really nothing like this," she murmured.

"No."

The nearness of her flesh had begun to work magic on Malone. He didn't want to scare her off, and really he was afraid of breaking her. She was even thinner than he had imgained. Her breasts were a pair of very small peaches, with prominent nipples. He ran a hand down along her buttocks. Small, very firm, he could almost have collected them in one hand.

"You shouldn't—"

His hand fell away at her small objection. He closed his eyes again and leaned back, feeling her flesh against his, feeling his hopeful erection squirm and flood with blood.

She was very still, and then he felt her shift slightly, felt her breath against his face, felt the tentative touch of her lips against his forehead.

112

Still, Malone did not move. Her hands rested on his chest now, and he felt her damp hair against his cheek as she kissed his mouth. He put an arm around her shoulder, but she shrank away from it, so he lay back again.

Every move from Malone resulted in Clara's shrinking away, but as long as he held still she was content to touch him, to explore his body. And a very nice bit of exploration it was.

Her lips crossed his chest, and abdomen, and her head burrowed between his legs as she kissed his inner thighs. Her small hands crept toward his sex, found it, and cradled it tenderly.

Malone hardly breathed. She had turned slightly and he felt her hip against his side, felt the delicate, unskilled probing of her hands, her breath against his sun-warmed flesh.

Slowly her hands kneaded him, running the length of his shaft with delicate uncertainty. She turned her lips to his again, kissing him harder, and he heard her breathing become ragged.

Clara lay beside him, still manipulating him, still kissing his mouth. Now she thrust against him; he was aware of the scrubbing of her pelvis against his thigh as her hand increased its tempo. His head had begun to pound with eagerness, and he let a hand drop onto her shoulder. This time she did not pull away from it and he let his other hand find her breasts, brushing his palm across the taut nipples. She shuddered, but instead of withdrawing, she pressed against him this time, her lips tasting his ear, eyelids, the tip of his nose.

Slowly, in some ritual known only to Clara, she readied herself and rolled onto her back. She drew him to her by the most convenient handle she could find, and settled him into her warmth.

Fragile she was, small and dainty, but Malone found out now that she had a wiry strength and a determination he had seldom seen matched.

As he sank into her to the hilt, she began to drive against him, writhing, sucking at his shoulders and chest with her small mouth. Her hands had formed into tiny fists, and she alternately flailed at the air and drummed on Malone's back as he rocked against her. She locked her wiry legs around his hips and shook him like a terrier shaking a slipper. She rolled and pitched, and it was all Malone could do to stay aboard; keeping up with her was impossible.

Some vital well of energy had been touched in her, and it welled up and then burst in a flood of enthusiasm. She muttered to herself constantly, clawing at Malone's back, going at him tooth and nail, as if he were something to be devoured. He thought for a frightening moment that she was having some sort of fit, but the spasmodic jerking faded to a soft ebbing and flowing, and Malone swam very neatly through this gentle tide, bringing a soft, nearly frightened series of sobs from Clara's throat before he reached a longed-for climax.

They lay there silently for a while, catching their breath, and then Clara rolled over, thrusting her buttocks up at Malone, her head resting on her crossed forearms.

Malone was never one to argue with a lady, and so he came at her again, and again her body reached an amazing, trembling zenith before she began her cooing, her satisfied, slow finish.

They lay side by side in the sun, the buffalo the furthest thing from their minds. It was then that Clara's hand slipped between Malone's hard-muscled thighs and she whispered into his ear.

"That!" he said with astonishment. "A rattle? I'll be damned. Clever, those Indians. I'll bet," he added, "the buffalo don't think much of the idea."

She chirped, a tiny laugh, and lazily rolled onto her back. Malone's mouth went to her breasts and he let his tongue tease her nipples. Her hands held his neck, toyed with his hair. She shifted again and, without speaking, urged him to try again.

114

"You're amazin' strong for a little gal," he said. "Amazin'." But he was up to it, and again he mounted her, riding her swaying body through the sun-warm day, letting the buffalo count themselves.

Schotte stood on the hillcrest, shading his eyes, puzzlement creasing his long face.

"I can't see them," he told Holzer.

Holzer stood in imitation of Schotte, looking Indian-style out across the slough.

"I can't see them," Holzer echoed.

"Clara!" Schotte shouted, then again, "Clara!"

Her answer came after a time—a sleepy, faint response. "Be up soon."

"Where are you?"

"Down here!" she called, telling him absolutely nothing.

"Is Malone there with you?" Schotte demanded.

"I'm here," Malone called from somewhere in the rushes.

"Damnedest behavior," Schotte muttered under his breath. Then, loudly, he called, "How many humpies?"

"What's that?" Clara called back, her voice still thick and dreamy.

"How many humpies?" he hollered, emphasizing each word.

"Three!" Malone called back. "So far."

Then, quite distinctly, Schotte heard Clara giggle. He put his hands on his hips, glancing in exasperation at Holzer, and yelled, "Say again!"

"Three!"

"No, four!" Clara called merrily.

"Mystifying," Schotte said, waving a hand. From where he stood, he could easily see two dozen buffalo. "I'll talk to her when they come up. It's mystifying..." He muttered something else and sagged to the ground, staring into space. Holzer sat as well, and he agreed with the doctor—or perhaps he was just practicing the unfamiliar word.

"Mystifying."

115

Holzer smiled and lay back, shutting his eyes. Schotte, able to think of nothing else to do, joined him, wondering silently if the long months on the prairie hadn't finally gotten to Miss Clara Marlowe.

nine ─────────────

Everett Haversham stood at the hitch rail, idly examining the town. Taylor had insisted on circling over this way after taking Haversham on a tour of the eastern boundary.

It wasn't much, even as frontier towns went. He was dimly aware of a piano, long-untuned, tinkling unmelodiously in an unpainted, false-fronted building up the street. A restaurant, a bank, a sheriff's office—apparently unoccupied—and a dozen tents fronted the road out of town.

He had seen two or three men from the post in town, so apparently it was a favorite spot for men on pass; why, he couldn't guess. Perhaps because it was the only place within two hundred miles.

Taylor came out of the telegraph office, squinting into the sinking sun. He untied his horse and nodded.

"Is that all?" Haversham asked.

"That's it. It didn't take but a minute, did it?"

"No." Haversham swung into the saddle, a little stiffly. He had done more riding in his few days here than in his last three months down in the Nation.

They turned westward, splashing across a narrow, sandy-bottomed creek, their horses' hoofes kicking up silver plumes of water.

"Couldn't you have used the telegraph key at the outpost?" Haversham wanted to know.

"That's for official business only," Taylor reminded him. "Unless it's an emergency. I don't think this message qualifies."

"Oh?" Haversham was tempted to ask about the telegram, but he didn't want to be pushy. Taylor told him anyway.

"Sent a message to Denver. A reminder."

"To Matt Kincaid?"

"That's right. St. Regis Hotel, Denver. The telegram will be there before he is, I guess."

"Important, was it?" Haversham ducked to clear an overhanging cottonwood branch. It was the last tree he could see for miles toward the outpost.

"Very important." Taylor winked secretively. "He's bringing something back for me."

"I see." Haversham really wasn't that interested. Perhaps Taylor wanted him to play a game of questions and answers, perhaps not. Haversham was only interested in getting back to the outpost before dark, eating, and falling into bed with his Cherokee beauty, and so he said nothing else. He rode silently, listening to Taylor whistle with self-satisfaction.

This was a fair and colorful land, Haversham thought. The empty miles of yellow grass were flushed to pink by the westering sun. A vast flock of passenger pigeons winged past with a muted thunder of wings, going to some nesting ground. Great, humpbacked buffalo stood in dark silhouette against the sunset. A few streaks of crimson fire lined the purpling sky where clouds, twisted by winds aloft, caught the sunset. The air was clean, and the horse beneath Haversham moved easily. It was all quite beautiful right then, empty and vast.

And she waited at the end of the trail.

Perhaps she would be fresh from her bath. He could picture her beautiful face vividly. Those wide, black, teasing eyes, the full lips ready to part with laughter . . .

Taylor turned to say something to Everett Haversham, but he saw that the man's mind was far distant. His eyes shone and he wore a faint smile. Altogether it was an expression that reminded Taylor startlingly of the one Haversham had worn after his "vision" in the sweat lodge.

Taylor decided to say nothing, and sank into his own vision of himself and his Otard-Dupuy brandy, sipped from a crystal goblet, the brandy glowing with tiny tongues of fire. He sighed. Maybe it wasn't much, as visions went, but it would have to sustain him for a time longer.

There was still a touch of color in the sky when the two second lieutenants reached Outpost Number Nine, but this was rapidly being extinguished by darkness. The mess hall was alive with the clamor of supper as Taylor and Haversham rode slowly past, taking their horses to the paddock, where Sedge Carpenter took over, unsaddling and rubbing the animals down as the two officers strode wearily toward their quarters.

"You be around tonight, Everett?" Taylor asked him, and even in the darkness Taylor could see the answering, slow smile.

"Not tonight, Taylor. I'm a little tired, actually."

"Sure," Taylor answered. "Well, I'll talk to you tomorrow, then." He watched as Haversham went into his quarters, and then turned toward his own room, talking to himself as he went.

"What do you want to do tonight, Taylor? —Oh, I don't know, a nice ice-cold bath might be just the thing. —You ever think about getting married yourself? —Only at times like this, Mr. Taylor, only at times like this..."

While Taylor was involved in his monologue, which lasted all the way to his quarters and for quite a while after that, Everett Haversham quietly entered his quarters and closed the door, noticing that the lamp was turned low. The scent of Catha hung in the air. Faintly sweet, faintly earthy—alive and fraught with sensual promise.

"Catha!" he called, but got no answer. He wondered if perhaps she had gone to visit Mrs. Conway, and hoped she hadn't accepted a dinner invitation. This would not be a night for the captain's whiskey and army talk.

"Catha?" He sailed his hat to the faded, satin-covered chair left behind by some long-absent officer's wife, and began unbuttoning his shirt.

As he sat to finish the task, he noticed the flat, yellow envelope on the table, and he walked to it. Glancing at it, he saw his name inscribed in Catha's hand, and again hoped she hadn't made plans to dine with the Conways. He glanced at the brass-housed clock on the wall and realized it was suppertime. He and Taylor had come in late. She might have gone to the Conways alone.

He opened the note, smiling at the effusive salutation: "My dear, sweet, loving Everett..." He turned, walking nearer to the lamp. Halfway there he stopped, his heart pounding as the message grabbed at his throat.

He stood woodenly, reading the letter again, trying to make the words mean something else. He stood on wavering legs, his mouth suddenly dry, reading the last sentence again through a blur that seemed to have settled in front of his eyes.

"... and so, although I know it will make you unhappy with me, dear Everett, and Captain Conway too, I suppose, I have decided that it is an obligation I carry within me, like my Indian blood, and so I have gone to meet these savage brothers of mine with friendship and with the greatest of hope."

He read it again, groggily, shaking his head. Then, without realizing he was going to do it, Everett Haversham bellowed. A loud, anguished cry that could be heard across the parade.

He burst from the door, still holding the letter, hatless, his shirt half buttoned. He rushed to the orderly room and stumbled into the captain's office.

Fitzgerald was there, boots propped up, wearing the officer-of-the-day armband.

"For God's sake, Haversham!" Fitzgerald came to his feet, shocked at the drawn features, the rumpled appearance of Everett Haversham.

"Gone. Out there!" Haversham waved a hand in a wild gesture.

"What is that?" Fitzgerald asked, moving around the desk. Haversham still held the letter in his hand, and he glanced at it blankly. Finally he handed it to Fitzgerald, who scanned it, burst into a smothered series of oaths, and grabbed his hat.

"Button that shirt, Haversham," Fitzgerald ordered him, and he did so, numbly.

"She's gone, I think," he said faintly. "I'll need a gun."

"Come along," Fitzgerald said sharply. Haversham was unresponsive. "We've got to see Captain Conway."

"Yes." That seemed to bring him out of it, and he strode along behind Fitzgerald to the Conways' quarters.

The captain was at supper when Flora, smiling, opened the door. "How nice," she began, but she read the tight expression on Fitzgerald's face and her own smile faded. "Come in," she said.

Captain Conway glanced up expectantly, then stood, folding his napkin as he read the urgency on Fitzgerald's face, the unconcealed fear in Haversham's eyes.

"What's up, Fitz?"

"This, sir." He handed Conway the letter, watching his commanding officer's face stiffen and draw into a scowl as he read Catha's note.

"She didn't mean...didn't know," Haversham began apologetically.

"This isn't the time to discuss the right or wrong of it, Mr. Haversham. Fitz, rouse Windy, have Wojensky form a patrol—any idea which direction she would have gone, Everett?"

"None, sir."

Warner Conway shook his head imperceptibly. That gave them a three-hundred-and-sixty-degree area with a fifty-mile radius.

"Find out first of all if she has a horse. She undoubtedly does. Find out from whoever was on guard duty which way she went, if they noticed"—since it was Catha Haversham, there was a good chance the soldier on duty *would* have noticed—"and get back here as soon as possible with Windy and Wojensky. Better shake Taylor out too."

"Yes, sir." Fitzgerald was already out the door, and Conway turned stiffly to Haversham, who wore an expression that was at once apologetic and terror-stricken. There was no point in berating the man, Conway decided. Besides, Conway felt guilty about this himself. He knew it had been brewing; the woman had spoken of nothing else.

"They'll kill her," Haversham moaned. He slumped into a chair and buried his face in his hands.

"Sit up, mister!" Conway said sharply. Out of reflex, Haversham straightened immediately. The shock of military discipline seemed to bring him around a little. "Any idea where she intends to find these hostile brothers, Haversham? Did she ever talk about it at all?"

"No, sir. Catha really had no idea where to go. But I understood the area to be nearly secure with the death of Wraps-Up-His-Tail."

"It is, and that's a point for our side. We have no knowledge of any large hostile bands in the immediate area. Of course, that doesn't mean they aren't out there. Some of Wraps-Up-His-Tail's malcontents may still be roaming about." Conway added, "The important thing is to find her quickly, before she does have time to locate hostiles."

Haversham was ashen. "If she does, what would happen?"

"I couldn't say, Haversham. Not with a certainty."

He did not say what he feared. Fitzgerald was already back, and Captain Conway heard other footfalls on the boardwalk, rushing toward his quarters.

Fitzgerald reported, "Windy's down across the deadline with one of his squaws—I've sent a runner after him. Jefferson and Keene were on the gate. They felt bad about having let her go, but I reminded them that she had every right to take a ride, and anyway, she doesn't fall under military jurisdiction.

"Keene says she was riding south by west, as if headed for the agency, but since she doesn't know exactly where it is, I doubt that the agency was her destination."

"We'll check anyway," Conway put in. "Maybe those agency Cheyenne are hostile enough to suit her."

"Hope so, sir. Wojensky's forming a volunteer party. With your permission, I told him two patrols—one led by myself, one by Taylor."

"All right."

"I'm going," Haversham said quietly.

Conway turned angrily toward him. "I know you're upset, Mr. Haversham, but that is not the way the military works, or don't you remember that?"

"I'm going, captain. Sorry. I'll resign my commission here and now if I have to do that to go, but I'm riding after Catha."

Conway held his silence a long minute. The young officer was deadly serious. "Ride with Taylor, Mr. Haversham."

He turned again to Fitzgerald, joined now by Taylor, who had just come into the room, still buckling his pistol belt.

"We'll have to ignore the eastern sector altogether. I doubt she'd head that way anyway. We'll work with a hundred and eighty degrees. Twenty miles out. In one day that's the maximum she could have ridden. Do you have any idea what time she left, Mr. Haversham?"

He shook his head wearily. "Keene says nine o'clock, sir," Fitzgerald put in.

"Almost a whole day's riding. All right." He moved to his desk, where he unrolled a map of the area. "Forget the southern quadrant too. That's agency land. If she went to the agency, no harm. If she rode by it within ten miles, the Cheyenne will have seen her. Send a rider to the agency, Fitz. Start him now."

"Yes, sir." Fitzgerald turned to find Wojensky at his shoulder. The corporal nodded his understanding and went to dispatch a rider.

Conway continued, "Since Keene says she rode south

and west, we'll assume she continued westward. I doubt she would have tried to trick us deliberately by circling wide. So forget the northern boundary for the time being. That leaves us with sixty degrees to the southwest and south. Twenty miles out, gentlemen. If you don't find her by morning, it'll be forty miles by nightfall. By the next day"— he did not look at Haversham—"there'll be damned little point in looking."

Malone saddled up morosely. The day had been a good one. Too good. He should have known the army would find a way to screw it up. A night ride after Haversham's missing wife. He glanced at Reb, who was leading his horse by, and past him at Dillson—why in hell the big man would volunteer for something like this was hard to figure.

Duckworth, eager for any action, was beside Malone. "There'll be a lot of riding tonight, huh?" the small man asked.

"Not so much," Malone said soberly. "Windy's not even here yet. When he does get here, it'll be a slow go. Windy's a good tracker, maybe the best *white* tracker I ever saw, but it's dark out there, Ducky. We've got a late-rising moon these nights. When it does come out it might speed things up, but not by much. Meantime, the Cherokee lady is out there having herself a little picnic."

"What are you so mad about?" Duckworth wanted to know. "If it wasn't for this, you'd be out counting buffalo again tomorrow."

"Yeah," Malone grunted, swinging up into the saddle. "But maybe I was starting to get the hang of that."

He hadn't volunteered for this, but Wojensky had his way at times. Coming into the barracks, Wo had told them, "McBride, Malone, Dobbs, Holzer—you're volunteering for a night patrol. Who else wants to volunteer?"

It was the only way Wojensky could avoid getting a patrol of all-green troopers, Malone knew; the old hands didn't volunteer for anything. Still, he didn't have to like it.

He checked the loads in both of his pistols for the third time and glanced wistfully at Clara Marlowe's quarters, where a light still burned. Oddly, he recalled at that moment a saying his Uncle Jake had been fond of uttering about thin women: "The closer to the bone, the sweeter the meat."

"You know, Uncle Jake," Malone said under his breath, "you weren't such a dumb old codger after all."

They were formed up into two patrols, Taylor and Haversham fronting one, Fitzgerald the other. Haversham's face seemed to have drained of blood. In the shadow of his hatbrim, his black eyes peered out of an ivory-white face.

Everything was being held up by Windy, who, having just returned from a difficult patrol, had taken the opportunity to visit one of his Cheyenne women across the deadline.

Windy claimed these visits were necessary to practice his Cheyenne and to catch up on all the local rumors. Malone wondered how much talking the old fox actually did.

A few volunteers had offered to go outside the gates and try to pick up Catha's sign, but Fitzgerald held them in check.

There would be less time wasted by waiting for Windy than by allowing the overeager amateurs to over-track the prints of Catha's horse.

"Here he comes," someone on the wall yelled, and within a minute Windy came through the gates, his horse at the run, his Sharps in his hand. He rode directly to Fitzgerald, and the lieutenant lined it out for him.

"Think she's going west, huh?" Windy shook his head and spat. "Folks down in the tent town think there's trouble brewing out there, Fitz."

"Trouble?" Haversham leaped his horse nearer. "What sort of trouble?"

"Some of Wraps-Up-His-Tail's bunch," Windy told them. "Seems they sent out some feelers, seeing if any of the local friendlies felt like kicking up their heels a little."

Haversham's face was drawn taut, his knuckles white as he clenched his reins. Fitzgerald shook his head slightly, and Windy Mandalian gave a shrug.

"That doesn't mean much, Everett," Taylor told him. "It's nothing new. It only indicates that they're a small force."

No one commented that it didn't take much of a force to deal with a single unarmed woman.

"Somebody get me a torch," Windy said, wheeling his appaloosa toward the gate.

Haversham followed Taylor and Fitzgerald outside, and watched in silence as Windy cast about for her sign. Finally satisfied, the scout got into the saddle and, over his shoulder, told Fitzgerald, "Off-hind hoof's wearing a built-up shoe. I can track her, but it'll be right slow."

They filed out, Windy with his torch leading the way. He didn't worry about finding every imprint the horse had made, but leapfrogged ahead, assuming that the woman, not trying to hide her tracks, would stick to the flat ground, not riding through rocks or brush unless it was necessary. They had made two miles when the moon suddenly shook free of the dark earth and rose into the night sky.

Windy snuffed the torch out against the earth, saving it instead of tossing it away. There might be other nights. A lot of them, he reflected unhappily.

They lost Catha's tracks in a sandy wash where hoofprints became formless indentations, and it took another hour before Windy picked them up a half-mile downstream.

The moon rode high through a glittering, cold night, and Everett Haversham followed in stony silence, knowing that their pace was incredibly slow, that with the dawn Catha would be riding again, and although they too could move more quickly in daylight, she was moving nearer to the hostiles with each mile.

He rode on in a daze, remembering when he had first seen her standing near the muddy river where the Cherokee women did their wash, her hands on her hips, a haughty, appraising smile on her lips.

He thought vividly of one other night, just before they were married, when they had spoken quite earnestly about the future, and Catha had urged him to study law or medicine, to work among the Cherokee, perhaps applying for the Indian agent's job. He had laughed, and the laugh echoed now in his ears.

"I'm a soldier, Catha. I'll always be a soldier, if I have my choice. It's not much of a life for a woman, I guess, but we'll be comfortable." He had held her close to him, the scent of her hair in his nostrils like the scent of spring flowers. "I'll take care of you, Catha. I swear I'll always take care of you."

Haversham's head lifted. The patrol had halted again and he saw Windy swing down, heard his dry curse as he relighted his torch and worked his way inch by inch across a vast field of stone. Haversham bowed his head and his eyes filled with unbidden, salty tears.

ten ───────────

She awoke with a smile and stretched her arms languidly over her head, shaking the dark hair from her eyes. She could not say what had awakened her—perhaps the mockingbird that chattered in the oak trees overhead, or the morning sun that sent flat, brilliant beams of light through the dark foliage, melting the silver frost where it touched the earth.

But Catha was awake. Awake and happy on this chill, clear morning. She rolled her bedroll up and tied it behind the saddle of her horse, which stood, head bowed, in the shade of the oaks.

Catha started a small fire, pleased that she could do it so easily with bits of dry, long-rotted bark. She watched the smoke spiral into the morning, and she brushed her hair before tying it back with a red ribbon.

She wore a divided, buckskin-colored wool skirt and a white blouse, with calf-high riding boots, yet she felt as naked and as blithely pagan as her remote ancestors on this morning.

The air was cool, the smell of woodsmoke haunting, touching in her an atavistic memory of warm campfires. She turned slowly, studying the empty plains; she might have been the only one alive on all the earth, to all appearances.

When her tea had boiled, she sipped it, walking in an aimless circle, kicking the earth with her boot heels, feeling impatient and exhilarated.

This is how it was, she thought. *This is the land of my red brothers. Children of nature, children of the wilderness. And masters of the wilderness*, she added thoughtfully.

She sipped her tea and chewed cold, salty biscuits, and found the meal immensely satisfying. She hummed as she broke camp, packing her teapot away. Only once did a fragment of uncertainty break her mood—when she thought of Everett, who was doubtlessly going about his duties concerned for her.

Catha shook that thought off. He knew how she felt, and the letter had made it quite clear that there was nothing to worry about. She had phrased it carefully, sensitive to his misgivings.

Once she was in the saddle again, even that concern drifted free. The broad grasslands spread out before her in an immense tapestry of promise. She passed nearly among a placid herd of grazing buffalo and saw, far distant, sleek antelope bounding away at her approach.

A quarrelsome jay followed her for miles, darting and squawking, and Catha laughed out loud. In the afternoon the wind rose, and she could see black thunderheads massing over the distant mountains, but that did nothing to dampen her spirits.

She was free and wild and intent on her noble mission. She was young, beautiful, intelligent, and dedicated. The world could not be darkened by a few clouds, nor chilled by the north wind.

She held the horse's nose toward the slowly sinking sun, and slipped on her coat. With a shiver of expectation, she thought that tonight she might actually eat her evening meal in an Indian village. Hopefully she scanned the indigo horizon, watching for smoke.

But there was none. Nothing at all for mile after empty

mile on the vast prairie, and with sinking expectations she began looking for a spot for night camp. The clouds that had been building now arced overhead like fingers of a dark, closing fist and she knew that it would rain.

Her spirits were somewhat lower, but not because of the weather. This was her second full day on the prairie and she had not met a Cheyenne. She rode on, aiming toward the shelter of a broken stand of willow and sycamore close by a dry steambed as the rain began to spatter down.

Not once did she glance back and see the dark, hunched silhouettes of the three men who sat their ponies atop a dark knoll, their eyes fixed on Catha Haversham.

Dillson cursed and rolled over. The india-rubber ground sheet beneath him had an unnoticed gash in it, and the water seeped into the two-man tent he shared with Malone. Lightning creased the darkness of the skies, and by its flash, Dillson could see the remuda of horses buck and rear in fright. A moment later, thunder rolled across the prairie, like echoing cannonfire, the ex-artilleryman thought.

The cold water puddled beneath Dillson and he could find no way to stay out of it. Angrily he threw his blanket aside and Malone rolled over, eyes alert.

"What is it?"

"Damned ground sheet leaks," Dillson groused.

"Oh." Malone rolled away, pulling his blanket up over his shoulder. He never awoke in the middle of the night without first thinking of hostiles, ever since that first time out with Easy Company—the night George Marsh had been scalped in his sleep. Something had chased the hostiles away, perhaps a night guard walking too near, and Malone had not been touched.

But he had awakened and thumped Marsh's shoulder, trying to rouse him, and finally, he'd drawn back the blanket to find the mutilated, open-eyed corpse. That an Indian could scalp the man asleep next to him—could have scalped Malone instead, as far as that went—that memory had given Malone permanent insomnia when on patrol.

He had slept with a pistol in his hand until he heard a

tale of a trooper in the Seventh shooting his own foot off during a dream.

Now he slept with an empty hand, but lightly, very lightly.

"I guess you knew it leaked," Dillson said sullenly. He was seated now, crosslegged, hands draped over his massive knees.

"What?"

"I guess you knew the ground sheet leaked, that's why you took that side."

"Shut up, Dillson," Malone muttered.

"Shut up? Oh, I forgot you're the tough one, aren't you, Malone?"

Malone didn't answer. He was cold and tired, and he only wanted to sleep. To sleep without recalling George Marsh, without feeling the stirrings in his loins for Clara Marlowe, who was probably now sitting, looking out at the rain, perhaps totaling humpies in her little book.

Dillson mistook Malone's silence for fear. He was a natural bully, had always been one, even as the fattest, dirtiest boy in the dirty coal-mining town of Youngstown, Ohio.

He had fought and blustered his way across half the country, trying to drain out some deep, poisonous hatred he carried with him like a cancer. He couldn't have told you whether he liked being a bully, a cruel and vicious brawler; it was simply the way he was now, evolved out of a vicious, dirty little boy whose tricks had included setting the Presbyterian church's organ on fire, riding his goat cart through melon patches, and leaving a dead chicken in his teacher's desk. Finally, inevitably, he had graduated to more serious crime. From an early age, his personality had been marked by cynicism and cold malevolence.

The army had changed none of that. The only part of army life he had ever enjoyed was manning the big guns. During the War he had, with immense satisfaction, nearly blown an entire village apart —churches, town hall, school, blacksmith shops, and farm houses.

Now they had taken that small pleasure away. He was

131

reduced to the rank of private, forced to live with the likes of Malone and Baby Ducks, as he now termed Duckworth. Stinking of horses and buffalo chips.

Dillson had worked himself into a heated frame of mind.

"I said you knew goddamn well this ground sheet was going to leak over here." Malone said nothing and Dillson, his voice lifting to ring out above the distant thunder, demanded, "Didn't you!"

"Sure, sure," Malone muttered from behind his blanket. "Now go to sleep."

"Damn you, Malone!"

And then he did it. He grabbed Malone by the shoulder, which any man in Easy Company could have told him was a bad notion.

Malone came up out of his bed like a scalded bobcat, roaring with anger. He winged a wild right at Dillson's bulldog head, but Dillson ducked and it glanced off the big man's skull.

Reb McBride was walking night guard, and he saw the tent explode as if a dynamite charge had been touched off. The two men came to their feet and the tent popped from its stakes, enclosing them in a cocoon.

McBride rushed for it, then halted in the rain, a half-smile on his lips. The tent bulged suddenly here and there as a head moved, a shoulder lunged, a fist glanced off the fabric.

Fitzgerald was awakened by the first roar from Malone's throat, which had sounded clearly above the rush of the silver rain. He popped from his tent, his Scoff in hand. Then he saw McBride standing near the tent in the darkness and the driving rain, and Fitzgerald slowed himself, realizing that the hostilities were confined to two of his own men.

Inside the tent, Malone lowered his chin, protecting his throat, and buried his forehead in Dillson's shoulder, hooking short, savage blows to the big man's ribcage.

The tent was draped around them and there was no room to maneuver, to step back, to dodge, but that had never been Malone's style of fighting anyway. He simply waded in, punching, hitting, and being hit until either he or his adversary went down.

Dillson was the same sort of fighter, with a few refinements. He butted, went for the eyes, and threw a knee up sharply, trying to bury it in Malone's groin.

Malone crossed a knee over, however, and Dillson's blow was deflected. The two men stood head to head, exchanging punches in the tight quarters. Malone overhanded a sharp left that caught Dillson on the ear and started the blood flowing. Before he could bring his guard up, Malone followed with another left, which stung the big man, glancing off his temple.

Muttering curses, Dillson fought back, going down below and then coming up with a damaging uppercut that slammed Malone's head back sharply, filling his mouth with salty blood.

Malone kicked out, trying to break Dillson's kneecap, but he tripped instead and toppled over, clutching at Dillson. Together the two men slammed to the earth, the tent going with them.

Malone found himself beneath Dillson. The big man was pounding his ribs with short, triphammer blows that drove the breath from Malone's lungs. A solid right crushed Malone's nose, and blood spewed from it.

Now Malone drove both fists into Dillson's face, and as the big man withdrew, Malone's heels came up and hooked Dillson under the chin, lifting him back and up, off Malone's chest.

Dillson's head rocked back and slammed into the muddy ground, and Malone crawled on top of him, his knees on Dillson's shoulders. Both of their heads protruded from the crumpled tent now, and Malone was vaguely aware of the rain on his shoulders, of the dark shadows clustered around them, but his attention was on Dillson.

With a barrage of lefts and rights, Malone hammered Dillson's face, numbing his own hands with pain as he slammed the blows home against Dillson's skull.

That skull must have been three inches thick, because Dillson took the blows and came back, throwing an effective blow to Malone's heart, a second to the liver, which set the lights blinking in Malone's head.

He went temporarily limp, and Dillson threw him aside, coming to his feet clear of the tent. He kicked at Malone's chin, his foot just missing a jaw-shattering blow as Malone rolled aside and got unsteadily to his hands and knees.

Dillson kicked him again, this time catching Malone squarely in the ribs. Malone heard something crack, felt the breath rush out of him as a brilliant blue haze filled the space behind his eyes, as his stomach twisted into a tight knot. He was half lifted from the ground, and he rolled away, going flat on his back, the hulking figure of Dillson hovering over him, the rain sweeping his thin hair across his eyes.

McBride had seen a lot of Malone's fights, but he had never seen Malone quit, and he wasn't as surprised as Dillson must have been when Malone came groggily to his feet, his hands clenched into limp fists.

Malone was battered and muddy; blood from his nose and mouth trickled downward to be washed away from his face by the cold rain.

McBride was aware of Lieutenant Fitzgerald beside him, and he glanced at the officer.

"Stop it, sir?"

"No. Let it go," Fitzgerald said. "I don't think Malone would ever forgive us if we stopped it now."

McBride grinned. "Yes, sir." He turned his eyes back to the two men, who circled each other warily now. Malone wavered on his feet, but Dillson, McBride noticed, moved clumsily now, his feet leaden.

Dillson stalked Malone uncertainly. The man was tougher than he would have guessed. He had landed his best blows, but Malone was still on his feet.

Dillson started hesitantly forward, leading with a short left jab, but Malone merely sidestepped it and, with a quickness no one thought he had left, lunged at Dillson, throwing his shoulder into the bigger man's chest.

They toppled to the earth once more, Malone landing a hard, chopping right even as they fell. Dillson rolled to the side as he landed, but Malone was all over him, landing unaimed blows on neck, ears, jaw—and Dillson, who had begun rolling as a defensive measure, kept rolling, trying to shake the ferocity of Malone's renewed attack.

But Malone could not be shaken, and with a roar Dillson came to his feet, swinging windmill blows at Malone's head. Twice he hit Malone flush, but the force had gone out of his blows as his exhausted arms and shoulders turned to rubber.

Malone recognized this; a solid right landed on his jaw as he came in recklessly, and he hardly felt it. The sting was gone. The big man was beaten, and Malone, knowing it, laughed exultantly.

Dillson backed up, shielding his face, but Malone was giving no quarter now. He waded in, snapping Dillson's head back with two sharp jabs, then hooking under with a solid right below the heart.

Dillson staggered and Malone kept coming, working downstairs to Dillson's wind, then suddenly coming upstairs with a whistling right hand that landed solidly on the shelf of the big man's jaw.

Dillson went down into the mud like a poleaxed steer, then tried vainly to rise. Malone stepped back as Dillson got to his knees, his face caked with mud, his puffed and split face drawn with pain, but Dillson wasn't going to make it to his feet. Malone knew it and Dillson knew it. He simply flopped back down and rolled over to his back, taking deep, painful breaths of cold air, the rain washing his battered face clean.

Malone staggered away, his fists still clenched, hanging at the end of limp arms. He practically walked into Fitzgerald.

"Sorry, sir, personal differences."

Malone braced himself mentally for the raking he knew was coming, for the punishment Fitzgerald was undoubtedly devising. Instead, Fitzgerald glanced toward Dillson and nodded.

"Is this settled now?" Fitzgerald wanted to know.

"As far as I'm concerned," Malone panted. "The man's too tough to go through it again."

"Dillson?" Fitzgerald looked at Dillson, who was sitting now, hands clenched around his knees. Dillson nodded.

"All over," he said grudgingly.

"It's over as far as I'm concerned, too," Fitzgerald told them. He looked at their tent, which had been trampled into the mud, and said, "I guess you two have written your own punishment. You'll be sleeping out tonight."

"Yes, sir," Malone answered weakly. It was still raining and his head felt as if it had been set on fire and beaten out with shovels. His hands were swollen and fiery; he guessed he had another couple of broken knuckles to go with the matched set he was working on. His ribs ached with each breath, and he was so exhausted he could barely walk or see straight.

He looked at Dillson, feeling no triumph, no satisfaction, and then trudged to the tent and pulled his sodden blanket from it. He made a bed to one side and lay down in the cold rain to try sleeping. Surprisingly, it came, and he slept through the night. Dillson never moved; he simply sat staring into the night.

Everett Haversham crawled back into his tent. To him, the fight was merely a meaningless interruption of the long, sleepless night.

His thoughts were clouded with dark despair. No one had to tell him that the rain meant Catha's tracks would be obliterated. In the morning they would break into two patrols and fan out, looking for any sign of her passage. But they would find nothing—and Catha rode on, nearer to danger with each minute, while they huddled in their night camp.

The rain slanted down, and Everett Haversham's face was lighted momentarily by the brilliance of blue lightning striking downward through the gloom of night. He lay awake, watching the rain, urging the morning on.

eleven _____

When she awoke they were there. Four men standing in a semicircle, watching her. Catha sat upright, startled by their sudden appearance. Then she smiled and got to her feet. The Indians watched her with expressionless obsidian eyes.

"Hello," she said, hoping they might speak English.

The men muttered together in a rapid, toneless exchange, and finally the tallest of them, a man with broad features, a broken nose, and a new Henry repeating rifle, took a step toward her and replied.

"Hello, woman."

As he stepped nearer, she could smell the rankness of his hair coat and the bear fat he had rubbed onto his body. His hair was heavy with fat as well, cropped off in a straight line. He was not Cheyenne, but Catha couldn't guess what he was.

"Where did you come from, woman?" he asked almost indifferently. He looked beyond her, across the prairie, where low clouds scudded over the golden grass.

"From the outpost," Catha said with a sense of confidence that was only slightly shaky.

"Who are you?" he demanded with a harshness that surprised Catha. He took another step nearer, and he was far from indifferent now, as he appraised her, his eyes sweeping over her breasts, her hips, returning to her beautiful face. She attempted a smile.

"I am Catha, a Cherokee woman. My husband is a soldier."

The man turned and muttered across his shoulder. She understood nothing but the word *Cherokee*.

"What do you want here, Cherokee woman?" As he asked this question, he prodded her bed with the muzzle of his rifle. One of the others had slipped from his pony's back and was now going through Catha's saddlebags. He hoisted a silky garment and grinned, saying something she could only guess the meaning of.

"I have come to visit my brothers, to learn your ways, to talk with you."

"To talk?" The big man said something to his friends, and they laughed.

"I am Stone Calf, Cherokee woman. I am Arapaho. What is your name?"

As he asked, he walked slowly around her, touching her hair.

"Catha," she said with a smile. "Is your camp far from here?"

"You want to go to our camp?"

"Yes. I want to talk with you, as I've said. I want to tell you why it is necessary that you lay down your guns. I want to tell you how the Cherokee have made their peace."

The man at Stone Calf's back spat and muttered something. Stone Calf translated, "He says the Cherokee are *all* women. Old women."

"No." Catha laughed again, but this time it was forced. These men eyed her in a way she did not care for, and for the first time she felt a tremor of fear. But, she told herself, it was only their way—bravado and ruthlessness to cover up their softer emotions.

"Maybe it rains again," Stone Calf said. "I think it is best to ride." He was not looking at the clouds, however, but eastward, toward the distant outpost.

There was only a moment's hesitation before Catha agreed. She mounted her horse and followed Stone Calf westward, toward the broken, hilly country where the Arapaho had made his camp.

As they rode, Stone Calf asked her, "Your husband is a soldier, Cherokee woman?"

"Yes. We've just arrived from my home in the Indian Nation."

"He was at the battle with Wraps-Up-His-Tail?"

"No. That happened just before we arrived."

"I was there," Stone Calf said. He thumped his chest. "I killed six white men," he bragged. That was obviously a lie, but Catha nodded respectfully.

"I can imagine that you are very brave, Stone Calf."

He was silent for a time. The day had grown cool. The clouds lowered their heads once more. The long grass fluttered in the wind.

"How many men has your soldier husband killed?" he demanded quite suddenly.

"I don't think Everett has ever killed a man, and if he did, I'm sure he would regret it."

"A soldier!" Stone Calf grunted with disgust. "I have killed many whites, many enemies. I have killed many white women, many children," he said, leaning toward her, awaiting her reaction. She shook her head slowly and looked at him.

"But why?" Catha wondered.

Stone Calf shrugged. "I do not want them here, on my land."

"I thought the Arapaho land was far south."

"This is my land as well," Stone Calf said heatedly. "Wherever I ride. It is all Indian land."

Catha latched onto that statement. "Because all Indians are brothers!" she said eagerly. Stone Calf only responded with a shrug.

"Not Sioux. Not Ute. Them I kill. Kiowa, when I was among them. Filthy Kiowa." Catha held her tongue, trying to formulate a new approach. Perhaps it would be easier in

139

the Indian camp. They would sit in a tipi and talk of war and peace, with Catha pointing out the obvious benefits of peace.

The rain held back, only here and there spotting the earth with huge drops of cold water. They were suddenly overlooking Stone Calf's camp, but it was nothing like Catha had expected.

No fire burned in the clearing below. There were no women, no children, no dogs, no tipis, only a single torn ex-army tent and a dozen men huddled under improvised lean-tos.

Stone Calf led the small parade into the clearing, and black eyes followed Catha from the shelters. He swung down before the appropriated army tent, and Catha got down as well.

Stone Calf simply dropped the reins to his pony, but Catha took the time to unsaddle. The warrior watched with impatience and amusement.

"Now. Come inside, it may rain."

Catha did as she was told, and Stone Calf turned to the other braves, barking abrupt orders. Stone Calf entered the tent and pulled the flap across the entrance, enclosing them in musty darkness.

In the corner, a spare rifle and a bandolier rested on a pile of tattered skins. There was a dried venison haunch in the other corner, but aside from those items, the tent was empty.

Without a word, Stone Calf walked to the corner and tossed his rifle aside, spreading out a bearskin. Catha watched him uncertainly before asking:

"Will I be able to speak to a tribal council? I do want to impress upon as many of you as possible the importance—"

"Be still, Cherokee woman!" Stone Calf snapped.

"I only wanted to assure—"

He stepped to her in two long strides and backhanded her across the face, violently, swiveling her head sharply. Her mouth filled with blood and she backed away from him,

140

touching her cheek. It was the first time in Catha's short life that a man had struck her. Her head still buzzed with the force of the blow.

Stone Calf gripped her arms tightly just above the elbows. His thumbs dug in so hard that her arms were numb. He shook her once, and her teeth clacked together.

"I do not care for peace. I will live like a warrior, die like one." His black eyes were blazing, his sour odor flooded Catha's nostrils. In panic she turned her head from side to side, her heart lunging into her throat.

Stone Calf released one arm and held her chin with a rough, strong hand. He pinched her cheeks against her teeth and told her, "If I were to council, it would be with men. With soldiers, not with silly women. Do you think the Arapaho care for the words of a white soldier's squaw?"

"Then why—?" *Why bring me here?* she started to ask, but Catha knew the answer without hearing it. Her eyes opened wide, flickering from the Arapaho's eyes to the bearskin that was spread in the corner of the tent.

She opened her mouth to scream, but Stone Calf slapped her again and her legs went wobbly. He turned and with one arm, as if she were a child, flung her to the earth.

As Catha watched in horror, the Indian stripped off his shirt and then his breechclout. He stood naked before her, his eyes gleaming, his dark, prominent erection filled with desire.

She crawled away, a hand in front of her face, but Stone Calf had hold of her ankle and he drew her back onto the filthy bearskin, tearing at her clothing.

Her blouse, save the cuffs, came free in his pawing hand and his eyes opened with delight at the sight of her perfect breasts. As Catha cringed in terror, his face went to them and he bit at her savagely, his teeth flooding her eyes with pain as he tore at a nipple almost as if he meant to devour her.

Her head swam. A vertigo of helpless horror bludgeoned her need to fight back, to scream. A colorless, rancid haze collected in her consciousness and she felt Stone Calf's hand clawing at her crotch, his fingers trying to penetrate her.

Her legs were lifted and her skirt torn from her, and immediately she felt his oily body pressed against hers, felt his hand crawl up her thigh to spread her for his erection, which drove into her dry womb without preliminaries, and Catha shut her eyes, fighting against the pain and humiliation as Stone Calf rocked and grunted against her, flooding her suddenly with his satisfaction.

Under lowering skies, the search parties rode westward. Windy Mandalian rode with Taylor's patrol, which included Everett Haversham, Dobbs, Holzer, and McBride.

Fitzgerald, circling farther to the north, was doing his own scouting. His patrol included a sullen, battered Dillson, and an equally bruised and cut Malone. Fitzgerald regretted not using this opportunity to separate the two, but Dillson was an inveterate troublemaker, and he wanted him under his eye. He also wanted Malone, who, along with Wojensky, was his most experienced Indian fighter.

"Anything at all?" Fitzgerald asked Wojensky, who was already wearing a slicker in anticipation of more rain.

"Nothing north of the wash, sir." Wojensky waved a hand, indicating the path that his small party, made up of himself, Duckworth, and Rafferty, had taken. "It could be she got farther than we guessed before the rain, though."

"Could be. Seems unlikely, though, corporal. She's new to the area, I'd expect her to pick her way. No, she's come this far unless she veered northward, and we should be able to cut her tracks."

Fitzgerald's eyes lifted to the slumbering black clouds, and he prayed silently that the rain would hold off at least until dark. They rode across the grasslands in a picket line, each man absorbed in his ground search, alert for tracks, trampled brush, turned-over rocks. Every man except Dillson, that is. Dillson rode somberly, his expression unfathomable, eyes directly ahead.

Duckworth had excitedly reported sign once, and they

had ridden to him, hearts racing. No one was in high enough spirits even to laugh at the green trooper's misidentification of buffalo tracks.

Fitzgerald took a slow, deep breath. The plains spread out for hundreds of miles and a passing horse left no more than a hint of sign. His men were inexperienced, there was bad blood between several of them, and the weather was threatening. He only hoped Taylor's party was having better luck to the south.

Windy spurred his appy up out of the coulee. The weather was strange, humid and mild, which was not an incurious combination for summer on the plains, but a biting cold wind descended at intervals from the high clouds. A late mass of cold Canadian air, stirred up by the projecting spine of the Rockies. Windy, like the others, found it oppressive, and he was in an ill temper.

Taylor was waiting when he burst from the brush up the sandy bluff. "Nothing below, I take it?"

"Nothin'," Windy replied, without glancing at the wooden-faced second lieutenant sitting his horse beside Taylor.

"I figure," Windy said, "we ought just as well to swing north gradually, maybe join up with Fitzgerald tomorrow late."

"And your reasons?" Taylor inquired.

"That's a rough stretch of country to the southwest, Mr. Taylor. Even figurin' the girl ain't shy of it, there's not much chance of findin' a living soul out that direction. And the girl was wantin' to find someone."

Looking across Windy's buckskin-clad shoulder, Taylor could see what the scout meant. The land was flat, nearly denuded all the way to Corson Corners. It was an unlikely spot for hostiles to hole up; their camp would be on the flats, visible for miles.

"I was thinking we can swing gradually north," Windy went on, "and that'll bring us up onto the bluffs at Elk Creek."

"What's that?" Haversham asked, his voice cracking with emotion. The kid was trying hard to keep it all in check, but it wasn't working. "Why Elk Creek? You have a reason, don't you?"

"Yessir, that's right. I do." Windy spat a stream of tobacco juice and wiped his lips on his sleeve. "According to my informants, that's where whatever's left of Wraps-Up-His-Tail's band are. At least," he added, "that's where they wanted any new recruits to join them."

"Then that's the place!" Haversham said excitedly.

Taylor was silent. The decision was his, and Windy had implied his own thoughts by his tone of voice. By riding that way, there was every chance that they would actually cut in front of Catha Haversham. There was also a chance, and a good one, that they would be involved in a firefight, and this search party would be turned into an embattled, very small patrol.

He counted heads mentally, glanced at Haversham's worry-torn face, and then turned back to the scout. "Any idea how many men are up there, Windy?"

"None. Sorry, Mr. Taylor. It's your baby."

"What if Catha is up there?" Haversham shouted.

"What if she's not!" Taylor shot back. "I'd likely lose most of my patrol for no purpose. Your wife could be trotting merrily across the plains, her little dreams light and gay in her pretty head, while my men are getting butchered because of her!"

Taylor was angry, and he showed it. The anger startled Haversham, who perhaps for the first time realized what Catha's experiment might cost. He could almost see Taylor mentally balancing the risk: the life of one woman against those of his soldiers.

McBride, the acting squad leader, drew up beside Taylor. His picket line had come up on the rim of the coulee and there was nowhere to go. Silently he watched Taylor, as they all did. Abruptly, slapping his own horse hard on the flank, Taylor told Reb, "File north, McBride. Inform every-

144

one that we are definitely in hostile territory now. I want those rifles across the saddlebows."

Darkness was fast overtaking Fitzgerald's patrol, and he was facing much the same decision as Taylor. They were getting close to those foothills behind Elk Creek. They had meager provisions and were a hell of a long way from the outpost. Taylor was far to the south, and if it rained again they would never find that woman. He thought of her beautiful face, her perfect figure, and he was able to curse her for causing this. Simultaneously he felt vast pity for her, and he shared with Captain Conway a certain feeling of guilt; one of them should have been able to get through to her, to shake her until she understood just what was going on out here.

"Lieutenant!" Duckworth's pointing finger lifted to the north, and Fitzgerald looked up to see Wojensky fogging it in, his horse's hoofes picking up the moisture from the rain-heavy grass, spinning clouds of spray.

Fitzgerald tensed, searched the horizon behind Wojensky, and he started riding forward to meet the corporal.

Wojensky drew up sharply, and his mouth was moving before he got his horse halted, so that Fitzgerald missed the first few words.

". . . half a mile. Five ponies riding west."

"Haversham's wife?"

"Absolutely. I'm no Windy Mandalian, but four of them horses are unshod, and the one wearing shoes has that built-up off-hind track."

Fitzgerald moved his men into a column and they rode silently and swiftly northward as the sundown briefly streaked the deep black clouds with dull orange. His thoughts ran ahead of the horses.

They had not found Catha Haversham; they had only found her horse. It was open to conjecture whether she was alive and riding it. If she was, she was in the company of four hostiles.

There were only minutes of daylight left when Wojensky led them to the tracks he had found. Fitzgerald swung down, immediately satisfied that they were the tracks of Catha Haversham's horse.

He stood, looking westward, where the clouds blended with the onrushing night, and he knew the woman was in desperate trouble, somehow knew that Catha Haversham was alive on this night, and that in all likelihood the Cherokee beauty was wishing desperately that she were dead.

twelve ───────────

He came again with nightfall, and this time he reeked of cheap whiskey. This time he was even rougher, pummeling Catha, tearing at her body, abusing her with his lust. She lay there stonily, her eyes open to the night-shuttered tent.

"What is the matter, Cherokee woman?" Stone Calf asked when he was done, rolling from her with a satisfied grunt. "You never had a man like me before, huh?"

She did not answer, and his hand suddenly shot out and yanked her head up by the tangled, dark hair. He shook her head violently and then leaned close to her.

"What's the matter, Cherokee woman? You lie like dead meat. No fun." He threw her away from him and she lay there, shuddering.

"You can fight, but you lie there. You are scared?" He hovered over her on his hands and knees. "Too much man for you, not like white soldier."

She did not speak or move; she barely breathed as he leaned his face closer to hers in the darkness. "You should be nicer to me. Stone Calf can protect you, keep you safe. Without me, it is very bad."

He sat up, crosslegged, and she glanced at him. *Very bad*. How could it be worse than it was already? She closed her eyes in misery, trying to picture Everett's cheerful face, trying to remember how lovemaking could be a joyful thing. She could not, and the tears that had not come all the time Stone Calf mauled her now rushed hotly down her cheeks as she thought of facing her husband again.

She was ashamed and frightened; and the shame was all the greater because Catha knew it was her own folly that had caused this.

How could she have been so stupid, so damnably stubborn! *Am I such a child?* she wondered miserably. She clenched her fists until her nails cut into her palms.

The night was long and cold, the ground beneath her hard. Stone Calf lay sprawled against the earth, snoring like a buffalo, and Catha remained unmoving, her eyes open to the bitter, bitter night.

The rain fell and she stood at the side of the road, a shawl over her blond head. From far across Denver, a train whistle bleated and a bell clanged. Matt halted his horse and turned back.

She glanced up at him, her blue eyes wide, her hands trembling, and then she simply keeled over. Kincaid swung down from the rented buckskin horse and rushed to her.

"Ma'am? Ma'am?" He shook her, but she did not move. He looked up the street and down, but this was an unfrequented avenue after dark, a business-district street, battened and locked after five.

He drew back her shawl and looked into her face. She was very young, perhaps eighteen, but very beautiful.

He hesitated again, looked around for a purse, anything that might have her name and address, but there was nothing. Thunder blustered in the roiling sky, and Matt scooped the girl up. She weighed practically nothing.

It was six blocks back to the St. Regis Hotel, and one flight up to his room.

The wind had blown the single high window in his room open, and so, after placing the girl gently on his bed, Matt closed that, shutting out the rain, although the wind still

148

shrieked in the eaves and bone-white lightning streaked the dark, tumultuous skies with occasional ferocity.

Crossing to the bureau, Matt dug through the drawers and found a clean white shirt. Taylor's venerated Otard-Dupuy brandy lay beneath the shirt, wrapped carefully in two boxes and several layers of newspaper. He smiled faintly at that and the remembrance of Taylor's wistful gaze, and he shut the drawer again.

Returning to the girl, he removed her sodden overcoat and unbuttoned her shoes. He shook her shoulders again, but she was still out, and so, with some reservations, Matt undressed her.

She was soaked to the skin through a frilly chemise, which he removed awkwardly, trying not to take advantage of the situation by dwelling on her naked body. But it was difficult; she was full-figured and lush with the firm flesh of youth. Her breasts bobbed free as Matt drew her chemise over her blond head, and he shook his head, taking a deep breath.

Finally he got his shirt on her, buttoned it, and stood back. It fit her like a tent, but at least she was warm and dry, not lying in the muddy ditch outside. He felt her forehead, but she had no fever he could detect. Gently he fingered her scalp, but found no bump or contusion.

Pulling down the sheet, he managed to roll her into bed. He covered her up again, drawing the blanket up around her chin, then, finding a cigar on the bureau, Matt retreated to the corner chair and smoked, watching over this golden little angel.

She slept peacefully and long. It was midnight before she stirred. Her arms stretched out, her hands in tiny little fists, and she murmured something. Matt leaned forward in his chair.

The girl rolled over and then came suddenly alert. She sat upright, her blue eyes wide, her golden hair in a tangle across her shoulders. She stared at Matt, raising an accusing finger.

"Who—who are you?"

She drew the blanket up around her throat as he stood. She watched him wide-eyed as he stepped nearer. Matt stopped and said softly, "I found you out along the road. You were soaking wet."

"Along the road?" She shook her head and gasped abruptly, her hand going to her lips. "Now I remember! Three men attacked us. My Uncle George—where is he? What's happened!"

"I don't know. I saw no one else."

She started to rise, but thought better of it and sank back on the pillow, her hair spread against it in a fine golden web. She bit at her knuckle and stared in childish fright at Matt.

"Who are you? How did I get here?"

"Lieutenant Matt Kincaid, miss. United States Army."

"You're stationed in Denver?" she asked, her voice timorous and small, so that Matt smiled in spite of himself.

"No, I'm down from Wyoming. I'm leaving soon, as a matter of fact. I was going out to dinner and I happened by. I brought you here and dried you out."

Her blue eyes flickered to the shirt she wore, and her expression was questioning. "Yes, I changed your clothes. Your dress was soaked through. I thought of asking the hotel maid, but I thought if they knew you were here, the management would raise a fuss. It wouldn't do for them to toss us both out in the rain."

"No," she said weakly. "It wouldn't. I am appreciative, Lieutenant—?"

"Kincaid. Matt Kincaid." He smiled again, and this time she reflected his smile, weakly.

"Matt Kincaid." Her voice was gentle for a moment and then rose in panic. "But what about my uncle! What have they done to him!" She started to get out of bed, but Matt went to her and put a gentle hand on her shoulder.

"We'll find out. Don't worry. In the morning we'll see the marshal. There's nothing at all to be done for your uncle tonight. Not in this weather."

150

As if to emphasize his words, lightning flared up brightly in the window and thunder shivered the hotel. The rain thudded down in torrential walls of water.

"You're right, I suppose..." Her head fell back against the pillow. "Anyway, I'm so tired. I was so frightened. Matt," she said softly, "you're a kind and gentle man."

Then she yawned and was asleep. Matt stood over her for a minute, studying her soft, quite beautiful face, the tiny hands emerging from the sleeves of his shirt, and then he walked back to his chair.

An hour passed and the rain drummed down. The lantern flickered and burned out, and Matt let it. He listened to the rain and smoked a second cigar. He heard her stir, and then, after a time he heard a small voice, seemingly distant, and quite wavering.

"Matt? Are you there?"

"I'm here."

"It's so dark. I'm frightened." There was a moment's silence as the rain washed down, and then she said, "I don't want to sleep alone, Matt."

He saw the flash of white, which was the sheet being drawn back for him, and he stood, walking to the bed.

"Are you sure?"

"I'm frightened, Matt. I've never been alone like this. I don't want to be alone now."

Silently he removed his boots and undressed, slipping in beside the small, warm woman as the storm raged on.

He was foul with sweat, and his unwashed mouth was sour. The rain had stopped, Catha knew by the absence of the incessant, maddening slapping of raindrops on the canvas of the tent.

She had slept only briefly, fitfully; but no dream had erased her knowledge of terror, and she awoke to it. Stone Calf crawled over her, forcing her legs apart, and he aimed himself toward her with his hand. She was stoic, although the tears fell—they seemed to come easier with each passing

151

hour. She did not resist until he tried to kiss her and that foul, scarred mouth found hers. Then she nearly gagged. She threw out a knee and screamed.

Far from discouraging Stone Calf, it seemed to stimulate him. He humped furiously, his throat filled with growling, grunting noises, until he finished, his scent ripe in the closed tent.

Then he stood, hovering over her like a dark, rank vulture. "You must make love back to me," he told her.

Catha sat up, her shoulders trembling with subdued anger, fear, desperation. She had no idea what he meant. Suddenly he yanked her to her knees, holding her by the hair, and she knelt before him, smelling the musky scent of his body, of her own.

"You must make it nice for me, or Stone Calf will make it very bad for you," he said in a gravelly purr.

But some strength deep within Catha had not yet totally surrendered and she tore away from Stone Calf. She came to her feet and tried to run, but he hauled her up short.

"You're a bad woman. I am tiring of your play, Cherokee squaw."

She spat in his face and he clubbed her savagely to the ground. She got to her hands and knees, naked against the floor of the tent, her ears ringing, her pulse swelling the muscles of her throat. She saw, without really seeing, the naked Arapaho warrior walk to the tent flap and throw it back. Outside, the ground was puddled with silver mirrors. The air was clean.

He's going to let me go! she thought with a rush of exultation.

Stone Calf stood in the doorway for a minute, his stocky body silhouetted against the gray day beyond the tent opening.

Then he turned and stepped across Catha. He kicked her in the ribs and she gasped, folding up, her head falling roughly against the floor. She crawled away from him, her hair hanging across her face, and he stepped behind her,

152

viciously kicking her between the legs so that she fell again, her spine aflame with pain.

She looked at him with hot, tear-filled eyes, got to a crouch, and cowered as he came toward her again. She threw up a protective hand, but the Arapaho slapped it aside. He backhanded her twice, roughly, and then took her by the shoulder, flinging her outside. She slipped, stumbled, and fell facedown into the mud.

She tried to rise, but could not just yet. All the same, through the blur of pain, the anger and humiliation, Catha felt a small surge of hope.

She was free of him! He had cast her out. Tired of her, he had thrown her to the winds. Somewhere out there, Everett Haversham, a kind, good man, waited for her. She had only to get to her feet, to run—or so she thought until she got to her knees and saw the other Arapaho men encircling her.

They stood grinning, their eyes coldly feral. The first of them undressed and Catha fell back against the earth, her mind a vortex of tangled thoughts. Anger was gone, hatred, fear. Only submission remained.

The first warrior ground his face against her breasts and spread her legs. She lay there, eyes open to the gray clouds, seeing nothing. A second man came, and then a third, but they might have all been the same, for all the difference it made.

She lay dazed, some rubbery male body on top of her, her mouth open slackly, her eyes blank. Suddenly she heard a horseman approaching. He swung down as his pony slid to a stop, and rushed through the camp, his voice high, urgent.

The man on top of Catha left without finishing. Stone Calf burst from his tent and looked toward the hills to the west. Conferring hastily with his men, he sent them to their horses. Catha's heart skipped once, heavily.

They were leaving! Soldiers were coming. It had to be soldiers. She tried to laugh, but her throat had forgotten that

153

emotion, and a strangled cackle emerged, bringing Stone Calf's head around toward her.

His eyes were obsidian, as cold and black as an animal's. He had the reins to his pony in his hand, but now he dropped them.

Stone Calf came swiftly to where she lay and she saw a sudden flash of silver. His hand had filled with a knife, and he approached her at a trot.

Catha tried to rise but could not, and then she felt Stone Calf's body on top of hers. She looked up and saw his savage face, saw the gleam of the knife, and then saw him lower it.

She felt the cold bite of steel against her cheek, felt the hot trickle of blood as he slashed her face. Then he did it again, again, carving a hatchwork into her face. When he was done, panting and grinning, he picked up a handful of mud from beside Catha's head and deliberately rubbed it into the wounds on her face.

Then he was gone. She thought it had begun to rain, but she could not be sure. It could have been the tears that trickled from the corners of her eyes and ran down her cheeks into the mud, or it could have been the dripping of hot blood.

The earth was cold and damp against her bare back, the sky a tangle of black and gray. The sounds of the horses drifted away and Catha lay there, her eyes open to the sky, her fists clenched into tight balls, her ravaged body still and unmoving.

thirteen ‗‗‗‗‗‗‗‗‗

The lookout had warned Stone Calf in plenty of time, but the Indian had seen only Taylor's southern force, and as Stone Calf's band burst out of the wash, they ran head-long into Fitzgerald's patrol.

Fitzgerald's men, riding at the ready, their rifles resting across their saddlebows, got off a telling volley before the Indians had time to react. Stone Calf went down in that first exchange, a .45-70 bullet tearing half of his face away.

There were twenty warriors altogether. Half of them were down or wounded, their ponies scattering across the prairie. The others took to the heavy brush, and Fitzgerald sent his troops after them. He wanted none of them escaping this time.

Dillson had missed with his first shot, and it irritated him. Shoveling a fresh cartridge into his Springfield, he spurred his horse after the nearest Indian. Behind him, shots echoed among the rocks that studded the area.

The Arapaho took to the brush, his pony lunging forward through the mixed sage and sumac, and Dillson was on his tail.

Suddenly he was aware of a second Indian to his left, and he cursed as a bullet clipped his arm. Turning in the saddle, Dillson fired back, missed again, and snatched for a fresh cartridge.

His horse, bucking through the waist-high brush, sank a foreleg into a squirrel hole and went down. Dillson was thrown free, landing hard against a rock, his rifle flying from his hand.

The second Indian was bearing down on him, and he got to his feet, trying for the protection of the boulders stacked behind him.

A bullet whined off the rocks, dusting him with stone splinters, and Dillson ducked, firing back across his body with his Scoff.

The Indian veered off and Dillson sent another searching shot into the brush. Rifle fire sprayed the rocks around him, and he began clambering upward.

In another second he knew he had made a mortal error. The Indian he had been chasing appeared above him and thrust out the muzzle of a Henry repeater. Three quick shots sprayed the rocks beneath and beside Dillson, and then he felt a sudden surge of fiery pain in his arm.

His Schofield dropped free of his hand and he toppled backward, holding his broken arm as the Indian above fired again.

He thudded against a round, grayish boulder and fell into a crevice between two slabs of stone. The Indian in the brush below fired twice as Dillson tried to stick his head up to find his lost pistol.

He ducked quickly, burying his head under his arm as the jagged ricochets flew around the enclosed area. He sagged back, trying to tie his shattered arm. It leaked blood profusely, and he had to grit his teeth with the pain.

You're dead, Dillson, he told himself. There was a hostile above him on the rockpile, and one in the brush below. He had no gun and he couldn't run. He could only sit there with the life bleeding slowly out of him.

From far away drifted the sounds of sporadic firing. Too far away. None of them would miss him anyway, he thought gloomily. Or care. Hell, they'd probably give the Indians a medal.

Once again, tentatively, he lifted his head, drawing a shot that was all too close, and he gave it up, pressing back into the corner of the narrow crevice, the pain throbbing in his arm, rumbling in his brain.

"He's alive, I saw his head again!" Duckworth said excitedly.

Malone glowered. "Up in them rocks?"

"That's right." Duckworth's face was flushed with excitement. "We'd better get him out."

"Get him out?" Malone laughed. He stood beside his horse, listening to the firing behind him, watching the brush ahead of him. "There's two of them hostiles, you know."

"There's two of us," Duckworth replied.

"Hell, yes, but they've got position. Don't the idea of going down there scare you just a little?"

"You're damn right it does," Duckworth answered. But his jaw was set with determination.

"That's Dillson, you know," Malone said, lifting an eyebrow. Duckworth only nodded. Malone took a deep breath. "Okay. You sit up here, kid."

"I'm not scared to go down."

"Nobody said you were. Can you hit anything with that rifle?"

"I almost made marksman once."

Malone looked to the skies for help. "All right. Here." He handed Duckworth his own rifle. "Keep both of them ready."

Malone stepped into the saddle, drawing his pistol. He looked once again at Duckworth, nodded, and spurred his horse into a long run down the grassy knoll. A rifle barked from the rockpile and an answering shot came from the brushy ravine.

Malone slid to the side of his horse, using it as a running shield. He snapped off two shots from under the horse's neck and then felt a bullet tag his horse. It went down headfirst, pitching Malone free, and he hit the ground hard.

Scrambling to his feet, he glanced up in time to see the hostile on top of the rocks rear up. Then he saw, simultaneously with the roar of a Springfield, a crimson smear appear on the Indian's chest.

The Arapaho slid down the rocks, his rifle clattering free, and Malone dashed for the boulders, rifle fire kicking up mud at his heels. He dove for the rocks and rolled behind a horse-sized, nearly square boulder, where he sat panting, poking fresh loads into his Scoff.

He waited a minute while his heart slowed its pounding; then, looking for reassurance to the knoll where smoke still rose above the prone figure of Duckworth, he made a lunge for the next boulder.

He was able to move behind them for the most part, although twice he had to expose himself, and each time shots from the brush sang past his ears.

He was suddenly over the crevice, nearly stepping into it accidentally, and he saw the crumpled blue figure in the shadows.

Malone leaped in and Dillson's battered, pale face came around. He had a rock clenched in his good hand.

"I'm no Indian," Malone said with a grin. Dillson's hand unclenched and he dropped the rock.

"What are you doing here?" Dillson asked, his mind unbelieving. "You—comin' after me?"

Malone grumbled a response. "Hell, you're Easy Company, ain't ya?"

Dillson had botched the job of tying off his bleeding arm—it couldn't be done very well with one hand—and so Malone removed the old tourniquet and fashioned a new one using his bandanna.

Dillson watched him the entire time with out-and-out befuddlement. He never said a word, even though Malone knew he had hurt him with his doctoring. Tearing off his shirttail, Malone made a hasty sling and knotted it around Dillson's neck.

"Now we got to get out of here."

"We're pinned down pretty good."

"The man up top is down," Malone told him. "Now for the other one." He took a breath and poked his head up. Instantly a bullet slammed into the rock near his head and ricocheted off angrily. A second shot, from a distant weapon, followed on the heels of that.

Malone slid to a new position and lifted up again. Duckworth was waving with his hat from the knoll, and Malone waved back.

Holstering his pistol, he slid back into the crevice. "Let's go—he got him."

"Who got him?" Dillson asked.

"Duckworth."

"Baby Duck?"

"Duckworth," Malone said without expression. He stood, hands on hips, looking at Dillson for a long moment, then he said, "Come on, let's get the hell out of here."

He threw Dillson's good arm across his shoulder and hefted the big man to his feet. Then they half walked, half slid down the rockpile to the ground. When they got there, Duckworth was waiting, smiling. Dillson smiled back; it was the first time he had used that expression in a long while.

"You'd best ride," Duckworth told him. "I'll walk with Malone."

Dillson objected, but it was only a small objection. He was weak and beat up. He took their help gratefully and clambered into the saddle. There was a lot of thinking to do, and Dillson did some as he rode, glancing now and then at the two men who walked beside the horse.

Fitzgerald took Wojensky's report as they rode into the wash. One hostile prisoner, the rest dead, Dillson wounded but making it, apparently.

He listened and was distantly satisfied, but Fitzgerald was hardly concentrating on Wojensky's words. The rain had begun to fall again. The wind whipped the drops nearly horizontally, and thunder rumbled.

They dropped down through the willow brush, which

159

was heavy with water, silver-green in the dim light. Fitzgerald spotted the camp, noticing the tent immediately. Then he saw the small, naked figure crouched in the mud and the rain, and his heart fell.

"Jesus!" Wojensky breathed. Even from that distance they could see her savagely scarred face.

Her dark eyes were empty as Fitzgerald swung down, taking a blanket from his roll to throw around her. The rain poured down around them. Catha's wretchedly damaged face turned up to them; there was no intelligence in her eyes.

"Get her out of the rain, at least," Fitzgerald said, hearing the unsteadiness in his own voice.

"There's a tent we can use, sir," Wojensky took Catha by the shoulders. "Come on, ma'am, let's get into the dry tent."

Her eyes shuttled that way, and Wojenksy felt her go tense beneath the blanket.

"No! My God! Not again, no!" she shrieked above the roar of the rain. The words fell away to a whimpering, subhuman sound, and Wojensky stood facing Fitzgerald in the rain. It was difficult to tell, but Fitzgerald thought there were tears in the corporal's eyes.

It was not so difficult to tell about his own tears. The rain flooded them away as quickly as they formed, but there was an instant's warmth in each eye before the cold water swept them from his cheeks.

At the sound of approaching horses, Fitzgerald's head came around. He saw Windy first and then Taylor.

Abruptly he saw Everett Haversham, and at the same moment Haversham saw his wife. He leaped from his horse, slopping through the mud like a madman. He circled Catha, and when he saw her face, his expression was that of a man who has been hit with a sledgehammer.

He slumped to his knees, his mouth hanging open, his eyes tightly closed. As the soldiers watched, he reached for her head, but she drew away, and after another moment Haversham got to his feet, turned his back, and walked

160

away, disappearing into the falling rain. Catha simply knelt there in the center of the clearing, encircled by mounted soldiers, her head hung to hide her face as the silver rain cast a shroud around her.

fourteen ─────────────

It was bright and warm in the small room. The sun beamed through the pale blue curtains and painted a bright rectangle on the floor. The atmosphere of the room was heavy and dark, however. There were corners where the sunlight never reached.

Captain Conway tapped on the doorframe, and Flora's head came around. He watched as she stood smoothing her skirts. He watched the sunlight in Flora's hair and he looked past her at the small, wooden-looking figure in the bed.

"How is she?" he asked in a low voice as Flora came out to the parlor. She shook her head.

"It's not good, Warner. Certainly not good. She won't eat. When she sleeps, it's a torment of nightmares. Her face will never heal, she knows that now. The mud those Indians rubbed into the wounds made sure of that. Such a savage act. And she was so beautiful."

Warner Conway took a deep, slow breath. He walked to the window and watched roll call for a moment before turning back.

"Is there anything we can do, Flora?"

"There's something a certain young officer might be able to do—if he tried."

"Haversham?" Conway's eyebrows raised.

"He hasn't been here, you know. Not since the first day."

"No, I didn't know that." Conway's jaw muscles twitched with disgust.

"Talk to him, Warner?" Flora asked, coming to place her hands on his forearms.

"I intend to do just that. And right now," he assured her. He kissed his wife's warm, smooth forehead, and then, with a single unhappy glance at Catha's closed door, he put on his hat and strode from the room, turning sharply toward Haversham's quarters.

He rapped on the door. Getting no response, Conway entered. Haversham was sagged onto his bunk, sitting with his hands dangling limply over his knees. He needed a shave, Conway noted. There was no point in babying him; he was supposed to be a man and a soldier.

Conway said stiffly, "You no longer rise when a superior officer enters the room, Haversham?"

"Yes, sir, sorry," he mumbled, struggling to his feet.

Haversham's blond hair was rumpled, his uniform was a mess. There was little life in those pale blue eyes. Warner Conway strode to the far window and, with hands clasped behind his back, said, "You're a pitiful sight, Haversham."

Everett Haversham was shaken by the apparent insensitivity of his commanding officer. "Sir," he said, spreading his hands, "you know—"

"I know when a man is indulging in self-pity!" Conway interrupted. "What the hell is it with you, Haversham?"

"Catha—" he began miserably. Again Conway cut him off, verbally shaking him.

"A hell of a lot you seem to care about her! When was the last time you were in to see her?"

Haversham was fighting back the tears. He answered softly, "I can't, sir. Goddammit! I can't bear to see her like that!"

Conway was silent. He took off his hat, wiped back his hair, and turned to the window. "You silly, selfish bastard," he said finally. Haversham was too shocked to reply when Conway turned to face him. "You heard me, didn't you?

163

I mean it. The woman has made a terrible mistake. She's paid a terrible, terrible penalty. Who in hell are you, mister, to make her keep on paying!"

"I know, I know," Haversham pleaded. "But seeing her as she is now, as she always will be, I can't handle it, sir."

"I see." Conway nodded, and his mouth tightened with emotion. *"You* can't bear it. What about Catha, bearing it alone! Her beauty's gone, is that it, Haversham? Her beautiful face. Well, I can remember you telling me what a woman she was. Good heart, quick mind, good to talk to, good to laugh with—all lies, I guess."

Haversham started to protest, but the captain held up a hand. "That's what hurts you, isn't it? She was only a pretty bauble for you, a woman to strut around with. And you'd watch the heads turn, see the envy in the men's eyes, and think smugly, 'Sorry, fellows, I'm the one that's going to bed with her.'"

"You've no goddamned right to talk to me that way!" Haversham exploded.

"No? Isn't it true?" Conway's eyes raked Haversham until he turned away, face bloodless. "There's more to it all, son. She's every bit the woman she was before. Or can be—that's up to you. If you can't accept her, she'll never be able to accept herself. You might as well walk over and put a bullet through her skull."

Conway had taken his service revolver from his holster, and he held it out to Haversham. Everett's eyes opened in bewildered astonishment. He was immobilized by the bizarre suggestion, hypnotized by Conway's searing gaze.

"Go to hell!" Haversham said loudly. He slapped the pistol from Conway's hand and it clattered to the floor. He strode past Conway, and hatless, he went out the door.

Flora Conway looked up with a mixture of pleasure and surprise at the young officer who filled the doorway to Catha's bedroom.

"I want to be alone with her," Haversham said quietly.

"Of course."

Flora picked up her needlework and brushed past him,

closing the door behind her. Catha's eyes were on him only briefly from out of her savagely slashed face, and then she turned her head away.

"Look at me, Catha!" Haversham said, more loudly than he intended. "Look at me, dammit!"

Slowly her head rolled back and her dark, tear-filled eyes looked into those of her husband.

He was beside her bed, and he reached down and took her limp hand. "We have to look at one another—" His voice broke off into a sob. "We have to stick together, Catha."

Then his legs gave out on him and he went to his knees, burying his face in her bedclothes, crying hot, forlorn tears. It was a little while before Catha's hand stretched out and she placed it on his head.

The stagecoach swept in from the dry plains just as Everett Haversham and Catha were being placed in the ambulance for the long trip back to Fort Laramie.

Catha wore black, a black wool dress and a black hat with a veil, which nearly succeeded in covering her scarred face.

"I hate to leave you in the lurch," Haversham told Warner Conway. "I know it's not that easy to get a replacement officer."

"Don't worry about that." The dust from the arriving coach sifted over them. "What about you, Haversham? Plan to stay in the army after all of this?"

"We haven't decided yet," he admitted. "We've been thinking a lot about the Cherokee down in the Nation. There's a lot they don't have, you know. Catha thought maybe she could teach school . . . I thought maybe I could apply for the Indian agent's post. See what happens."

"You'd do a job for them," Conway said, shaking his hand. "I'm sure of that. Write and let us know how you're doing, will you?"

"I will." Haversham was silent, his eyes downcast.

"Do. I mean it."

"Thank you, sir," Haversham said. "For kicking me in the butt when I needed it, I mean. We'll be all right, sir. I know we will. We just need to adjust to it all. Time to forget. But we will be all right," he said with a forceful exhalation and a smile at Catha, who nodded back and said:

"We *will*."

Conway nodded, shook Haversham's hand again, and closed the door to the ambulance as Everett entered and sat beside Catha.

"I hope you will be," Conway said under his breath. He put his arm around Flora and they waved as the ambulance turned and rolled toward the gate, the dust rising in plumes. He looked down at Flora and she smiled—a bittersweet smile. Her eyes were filled with tears and he squeezed her.

"I'm ready for some dinner, woman," Conway said. He tugged his hat low and started for his quarters. Then he saw the lone disembarking stagecoach passenger and he waved across the parade.

Leaving Flora, he walked to where Matt Kincaid stood. Taylor, wearing a sober expression, had appeared to walk beside his captain.

"He's back soon, isn't he?" Taylor asked.

"He is. Must have missed the place." Conway thought of something else and he asked, "How's our other casualty doing?"

"Dillson? He's on the mend."

"Still want to return to artillery after all of this?"

"He says so, sir."

"Same old Dillson, is he?"

"Oh, no! He's changed completely, sir. He really has. Some of the burr's been taken off of him. By the way, there's another man who wants to be reassigned to artillery with Dillson."

"Another man? Don't tell me—"

"Yes, sir," Taylor said with a grin. "Private Duckworth. He's been nursing Dillson, and the old criminal has Ducky convinced that the artillery is the place to be."

Matt Kincaid stood with his suitcase beside him, watching the two officers approach him. He smiled and they shook hands all around.

"Good to be back?" Conway asked with a straight face.

"Always, sir," Matt answered.

"Cut it short, didn't you?"

"Yes, sir," Matt said, lifting his valise to walk with Conway and Taylor toward the officers' quarters. "I had enough of the big city. It really is good to be back to Number Nine." He looked around and added with a shake of his head, "Though I can't say why."

Conway said goodbye at the barracks door, and Taylor followed Matt inside. He sat on his bunk, watching Kincaid unpack, and finally he asked, "Matt, what really happened?"

"Is it that obvious?"

"It's obvious to me that no man in his right mind comes back to Number Nine when he could be kicking up his heels in Denver."

Matt stopped unpacking and threw his suitcase aside so that he could sit on his bed. "You're right, Taylor. I ran out of funds. I had to come back."

"So tell me about it."

Matt did, with obvious embarrassment. "And when I woke up, she was gone. So was my wallet, my pistol, my watch . . . and your bottle of brandy, Taylor, I'm sorry. I'll repay you, of course."

"Somehow it doesn't seem so important anymore," Taylor said with a shrug. "Thank God you'd paid your hotel bill in advance. That girl was good, wasn't she? Making sure she found out you were from out of town and would be leaving soon. And what a story—you should never have fallen for that, Matt."

"I know." He glanced up. "Sometimes it's so easy to believe what they tell you, Taylor. When they look like she did, especially." He smiled and then told him, "You know— for that one night—it was damned near worth it."

"I hope so. It cost you."

"Wasn't that Everett and Catha Haversham I saw getting

into the ambulance? Where in hell are they going?"

"Later, okay, Matt? If you don't mind, I'd rather not talk about it right now. Tell me about Denver. About the brandy, what shape the bottle was. And tell me about the girl. Tell me that whole sad, beautiful tale about the blond thief again."

Malone was reading the duty roster, and Rafferty said from behind him, "You and me and Dobbs. Dig a new latrine pit."

"Now there's a job for a man," Malone said laconically. A cold cigar dangled from his lips. He shrugged and rolled his sleeves up.

"Hell, I don't know," Rafferty said as they walked toward the tool shed, "it beats some work. Probably beats counting buffalo, I mean."

"Now see," Malone said, wagging a finger at Rafferty, "that is the voice of ignorance. That counting buffalo is a hell of a good duty."

"Maybe." Rafferty shrugged. "Though I can't see what the hell anybody cares about how many buffalo there are anyway."

"There you are again," Malone said, shoving his hat low across his eyes as they crossed the parade. "Rafferty, don't you realize how many things can be done with a buffalo? Now you take just the hides alone. From them you can make tipis, bedcovers, medicine bags, leggings, dresses, saddle covers, bridles, hobbles..."

Malone's voice faded away in the day, and the dust from the ambulance settled slowly. From across the parade the smith's hammer rang and from the kitchen the smoke rose into the clear blue Wyoming skies.

SPECIAL PREVIEW

Here are the opening scenes
from

EASY COMPANY AND THE BIG BLIZZARD

the next novel in Jove's exciting
High Plains adventure series

EASY COMPANY

coming in April!

one

Private Trueblood reached the end of the parapet along the stockade wall of Outpost Number Nine, and turned and yawned, glancing at the eastern sky to see that finally the horizon was lightening, that his night of cold, monotonous guard duty was nearly ended.

Trueblood yawned again and marched slowly back toward the gate where he had met Yount countless times that night as they turned around to walk the parapet again, like mechanical bears in a shooting gallery. The plains became slate gray, emerging from the darkness of night to take on form and substance.

A lamp flickered on in the barracks. That would be Reb McBride, the bugler, who was first up as a rule. Inside half an hour, Reb would be blowing sweet reveille and not long after that the even sweeter grub call.

Trueblood glanced toward the mess hall and saw the smoke rising from the stovepipes to merge with the dull gray sky, and his stomach gurgled with anticipation. All Trueblood wanted was a warm breakfast and a day's sleep.

He turned again and walked back toward the gate, holding himself a little more erect now that Captain Conway and First Sergeant Cohen were likely to be up and stirring, and glanced at the northern skies to his right.

He frowned and wiped his raw eyes. The sky was a deep, deep blue, almost blue-black to the north and northwest. It was an eerie, almost electric blue, of the shade they called Prussian.

He stared at it a moment, with interest, until he made his turn and the more compelling thoughts of breakfast and sleep returned to sweep away what he imagined to be a trick of sunrise.

McBride emerged from the enlisted barracks and blew reveille, setting the yawning, stretching outpost into sluggish motion.

Armstrong and MacArthur staggered toward the gate, reported to Wilson, who was corporal of the guard that morning, and relieved Trueblood and Yount, who clambered down the ladders from the parapet and returned to the barracks.

McBride had come out without his greatcoat. The days had been growing warmer lately, and he figured there was no need for such clothing. Now, following Trueblood and Yount back toward the barracks, he began to shiver. It was still damned cold, he decided. Or maybe he was getting older, the circulation slowing. Before grub call, he snatched up his greatcoat. He was glad he had; it was no warmer then, half an hour later, with the yellow ball of the sun cresting the low, dark horizon.

In the transient Indian camp to the northeast of Outpost Number Nine, Windy Mandalian strode from the tipi he had shared with Running Doe. The woman still slept, snuggled in the warmth of her buffalo skins and furs, drugged by a night of lovemaking.

The scout was not one for sleeping in, however; first light arrived an hour after Windy had risen, stoking the fire, filling his pipe, drinking hot coffee by starlight.

He felt it in the air. Dawn confirmed his suspicions. A blue wall moved slowly southward toward Wyoming, and

172

Windy turned and picked up his buffalo coat and badgerskin gloves before riding his appaloosa pony to Number Nine.

She opened a sleepy eye and looked up at her man. Tall, handsome, silhouetted by the faint light that filtered through the curtained window.

"I'll be up in a minute," Flora Conway yawned. "I'm sorry, I should have been up by now. I don't know why I'm so tired."

"Don't you?" Captain Warner Conway finished buttoning his tunic and returned to the bed. He sat beside his wife, enjoying the picture she presented—sleep-tousled dark hair, yawning mouth, nightdress unbuttoned still, hinting at the smooth swell of her breasts.

Flora leaned forward and drew his head to her breasts, kissing his forehead as she smoothed his dark hair with a gentle hand.

"Cold, isn't it?" Flora asked. "Or is it me?"

"It's chilly," the captain agreed. He felt her fingers running down the nape of his neck and he felt the stirring between his thighs.

Flora's arms encircled him and she whispered into his ear, "What time is it?"

"Why?" He glanced at his pocket watch. "There's not *that* much time." He kissed her lips and nuzzled her sleep-warmed throat.

"It wouldn't take long. Not this morning, Warner."

"I really don't think—"

Flora had begun unbuttoning her nightdress, a teasing smile playing on her lips.

"Flora..." he protested, but that was as far as his protest went. She shrugged out of her nightdress; her smooth shoulders and still-firm breasts were bared, drawing the captain's eyes, hands, lips.

"I'll be late," he complained. Already he was removing his tunic, however.

"There has to be some advantage in being commanding officer, Warner."

"There is," Conway said, slipping out of his pants and into bed. "I'm the man who has the privilege of sleeping with the CO's lady."

"They won't miss you for ten minutes," Flora murmured.

She had shed her nightdress, slipping from its sheer cocoon. Now his lean, hard body was against her, and she breathed with slow contentment as his lips surveyed her breasts with slow, lingering kisses.

She reached between his legs and cradled his swelling erection. She threw back the bedsheets as he got to his knees and let his lips run across her abdomen.

She clutched him more tightly now, spreading her legs as his kisses reached her inner thighs, sending tremors through her body, pinpoints of electrical current that ran from her crotch to her breasts, causing her nipples to tingle.

Her thighs parted and Warner's fingers explored the familiar, compelling warmth of Flora's inner flesh. Her scent too was familiar, but always intriguingly new. The button of flesh that lay nearly concealed in the soft, curly hair that flourished there was rigid, and Conway's fingers ran along it, tracing ovals, and Flora shuddered, lifting her pelvis.

Her fingers ran along the length of his shaft, pausing at the head of it to move around it in maddening, slow circles. Flora rolled toward him, her smile deep, her eyes bright, and Warner Conway lay back, placing his head on the pillow.

"What is it?" he asked.

"Nothing. Nothing. Lie back, dear. I know exactly what I want and exactly how to find it."

"In ten minutes?" he asked with a mock frown.

"Damned near in ten seconds." He lay back and she straddled him, still holding his erection. "The way you've got me excited, you brute." Her voice was low and breathy now.

Conway cupped her breasts. Her hair, falling free, lay across his chest as she bent forward to kiss him. Then Flora shook back her hair and lifted herself, touching the head of his erection to her crotch.

Conway's hands joined her there. He spread her gently, feeling her fingers, now moist with her own juices, and his sex, which pulsed and wriggled with need. Together, their fingers interlaced, they eased his shaft into her depths. Slowly she settled on him, slowly, her inner muscles rippling against him.

Conway's hands still rested there and his thumbs found her clitoris, moving in slow circles around it as Flora, sitting absolutely still for a moment, tilted her head back. Her eyes were closed, her throat muscles taut with sensual concentration. Her body pulsed against his and gradually she began to sway, to stroke against him.

Warner's hands slipped behind his wife's legs, crawling up the backs of her thighs to run across the soft curve of her buttocks. His finger traced the line of her cleft from the tail of her spine to where he entered her, his finger lingering there to touch the incredible softness of her, to feel her shuddering against him, encircling him.

She had begun to move differently now, to pitch against him, her pelvis grazing his. Her breasts swayed and her thighs quivered with the advent of a soft, utterly pleasurable climax.

He was huge inside her, filling her with joy, with need, and Flora murmured something nonsensical as she moved her hips in tight, demanding circles.

Warner clenched her buttocks tightly, lifting his own hips higher, harder, thrusting against her. Flora gave a little gasp and collapsed against him, kissing his ears, his throat, his chest as Conway, holding her against himself, worked toward his own draining climax.

She was soft and her lips were tender, her body demanding, and he folded his arms around her, coming with a sudden rush, deeply, passionately.

She lay against him and his hands ran down her smooth, narrow back, across the rise of her buttocks, returning to her shoulders. He held her head by the neck and kissed her hotly.

"Again?" she asked, her fingers running along his lips.

175

"My God, woman—some people are never satisfied!"

"I'm satisfied as long as I have you, Warner. But then, it doesn't hurt to ask, does it? We need a vacation." She rolled away, stretching. Her breasts rose with the motion. "We could spend all day in bed, like newlyweds. Remember Denver?"

"I couldn't get away, Flora. Maybe next summer."

"Oh, I know it." She yawned, then, with a determined nod, swung her feet to the floor. "But I like to daydream, to pretend." She sat beside him, her hand on his shoulder. She kissed his back and leaned her head against him.

Corporal McBride blew grub call, and Warner Conway nearly came to his feet. He was a methodical man, a soldier, punctual and practical, hardly a daydreamer. She kissed him again and sat watching as he dressed hurriedly.

"Breakfast?"

"I'll eat in Dutch's mess this morning," Warner said. "It *is* cold," he said, frowning. Conway opened the door to the black iron stove that sat in the center of the room, and poked some fresh fuel in—real wood, not buffalo chips. A privilege of rank.

Flora was in her robe now and she came to him, pecking him goodbye. She wanted to hold him, to cling to him, but over the years she had learned not to do so at moments like this.

There was duty, a clock on the wall, his men to care for. She stood beside the door as he went out, striding down the boardwalk toward the kitchen of Dutch Rothausen. Flora stood there until she could no longer see her man. Then, clutching her wrapper to her throat against the cold, she turned and went back into her quarters.

Acting Master Sergeant Ben Cohen, the first shirt of Outpost Number Nine, had the coffee going before Captain Conway had arrived at headquarters.

He snapped the captain a salute and blinked as the door to the office was banged shut by the rising wind. "Getting set to blow, is it, sir?"

"It looks like it, Sergeant." The captain, Ben noticed, had a somewhat distracted expression this morning.

"Feels funny out there, I noticed," Cohen said. "Makes the hair on your neck stand up." He poured coffee for his commanding officer and followed him into his office, carrying the opened mail, which he placed at Conway's left hand.

After leaving the captain's office, Sergeant Cohen poured himself a cup of coffee, stoked up the fire, rubbed his arms, and sat at his desk.

No sooner had he seated himself than the door, aided by the gusting wind, burst open and a grizzled, hulking man in buckskins and a buffalo-hide coat appeared.

Cohen glanced up without expression.

"Help you, sir?"

"You can indeed. I hope so, at least. Name's Cambridge," the big man said, without offering a hand. He closed the door behind him and tramped to Cohen's desk. Cambridge had a lean face, bulky shoulders, and a distinctive odor.

"I want to see the commanding officer," he said.

"He's in. I'll ask," Ben said. He wrinkled his nose and went to the captain's door. Rapping once, he entered.

"Man to see you, sir. Buffalo hunter, by the smell of him."

Captain Conway nodded, placed his mail aside, and stood to greet the civilian, who carried a rifle in the crook of his arm. As Ben had warned him, he had a ripe, distinctive aroma about his person.

"Warner Conway," the captain said, extending a hand.

"Cambridge." The buffalo hunter managed to unwind his hand from his Spencer rifle and shake hands. It seemed to be an unaccustomed civility with the man.

"Sit down, tell me what I can do for you."

"I don't need to sit. This is an emergency, Captain. I got a man bad hurt and I need to borry your doctor."

"We do not have a post surgeon, Mr. Cambridge," Conway had to tell him.

177

"The hell! No doctor on an army post!" Cambridge frowned in disbelief.

"I'm afraid we don't rate one, Mr. Cambridge."

"Christ!" Cambridge sagged into a chair. "I was misinformed then. The kid's gonna die, looks like," he said as if speaking to himself.

"What happened?" Conway wanted to know.

Cambridge waved a hand and sighed with digust. "We hired on a new skinner. Me and Bob Evers, that is. Just a kid he is, name of Harry Daley—not that it matters."

The buffalo hunter leaned forward and explained what had happened.

"Me and Bob Evers had us three skinners—Injuns. But one took off to make medicine, so we took on a green kid off a wagon train. Name of Daley. His folks was going on to Oregon, but they was some squabble—believe the old man wasn't his real daddy, I don't know." Cambridge shrugged. "He wanted to work and we took him on."

Conway had a nearly overwhelming impulse to get up and open the window, Cambridge was that ripe, but he overcame the urge.

Cambridge got on with his tale. "Thing that happened was the kid got careless. He was skinning out a big bull— and I mean a *big* son of a bitch, Captain. Put his knife to that damned bull's gullet and up he rose."

"The bull was alive?"

"He was that," Cambridge confirmed with a nod. "It happens. Evers just thunked the buff across the skull with his shot, you see. Bull went down, out colder than a mackerel, but hardly hurt. It's a skinner's lookout, but the kid was green. The experienced man will give 'em a good kick, make damned sure they're dead and not just down. But Daley, he got to his knees and stuck the bull, and the old buff came to his feet madder'n hornets. Daley jumped up yellin', but he was too slow. Time I unlimbered my rifle and put the bull down for keeps, he'd half tore the kid's leg off."

Cambridge took a deep, tense breath. "It's a bad one,

178

Captain. Thigh bone's all busted up, meat torn away. We got him trussed up and filled with whiskey to numb him some, but the kid's gonna die if the leg don't come off. Me and Bob, neither of us wanted to go after that leg with a skinnin' knife. Likely kill him our own selves. So I rode up here. Bob says, 'Ever' army post has to have a surgeon. It's in the rules.'" Cambridge shook his head. "But I guess it ain't so. You ain't a doctor, you cain't help us. I'll be going back."

The buffalo hunter rose heavily, his chair scraping on the floor. Conway stood also.

"I said we didn't have a doctor," Conway said, "but I didn't tell you we couldn't help. You hold on. I've got a man who can see to that leg."

Dutch Rothausen mopped his forehead with the back of his hand. Breakfast was over, but dinner was already being prepared. The KPs clattered the dishes together in the dish tubs, and the kitchen filled with steam. A dish slipped and broke against the floor.

Rothausen turned, his red face growing redder, and hollered at the guilty KP. Farnsworth, Dutch's assistant, was burning the beans, and Rothausen bellowed.

"Farnsworth, you fuckhead! Pour some water in these beans!"

Farnsworth appeared, trembling, and ducked away. Pots clattered against the floor. Rothausen looked to the heavens, his eyes rolled back.

Those beans had an awful smell to them. He turned around, frowning, and then saw the man dressed in a buffalo-skin coat, standing in the kitchen door.

"You Rothausen?"

"I am." Dutch ambled to where the buffalo hunter stood. A big man, he was dwarfed by Dutch's bulk. "If it's coffee you want, help yourself."

"Captain says I should see you. We need a leg taken off a man, down twenty miles south. Captain says you're the man for the job."

Dutch nodded. It was no new request. He estimated he had taken off more limbs than an average doctor would in ten years of practice. It was a skill born of necessity. "I'll be right with you," Dutch said.

He collected his meat saw, two large butcher knives and a sharpening steel. Snatching a bottle of brandy from the cupboard, he shouted to his assistant, "I'm leaving, Farnsworth. Should be back by supper."

"All right, Sergeant," Farnsworth said, not bothering to conceal the smile of relief on his face. Dutch could be intimidating with his bulk and low boiling point, and Farnsworth was intimidated.

Dutch stripped off his apron and stuffed it into the burlap sack at his feet, along with the implements and brandy. He watched Farnsworth spill water into the fire, and grumbled. He hadn't had a decent assistant since Torkleson left. "Don't burn the place down!" he shouted.

Then, grabbing his coat and hat, hefting his sack, Dutch joined Cambridge.

Second Lieutenant Taylor hunched his back against the rising wind. He had seen the skies at dawning and had not liked what he saw. Fortunately they were nearly at the perimeter, because, unless Taylor missed his guess, it was going to snow, and snow hard. With luck, however, they would be back at the outpost before it started.

Corporal Miller angled his bay toward Taylor. The three soldiers with him were buffeted by the rising wind, which turned their hatbrims back, lifted their coattails, and whipped the manes of their horses.

"Nothing, sir," Miller reported.

"Thank God." He nodded toward the northern skies. "We don't need any hostile contact now."

"If that's going to be as bad as it looks now, the Indians will be holed up," Miller guessed.

"That's just what *I* have in mind, Corporal."

Miller smiled. His ears were cold and his nose glowed. He looked out across the vast grasslands to the south and east. "What in God's name do they come here for?" he asked.

He referred to the settlers—or would-be settlers. At this time of the year, looking forward to a winter crossing of the Rockies, a few always turned north, off the Bozeman, with the idea of finding a patch of grass to farm.

Little Jack had been prowling this area until recently, and the renegade Arapaho was having a field day. Plenty fancy ribbons, plenty horses—plenty dead settlers.

Taylor answered, "I guess they're looking for something. What does any man come West looking for?"

"If they knew what it was like—really like—there wouldn't be many of them," Miller said.

Private Dobbs, Forrester, and Burns had arrived. They sat their horses, backsides to the wind, looking expectantly, hopefully to their officer.

"Let's get on back," Taylor said.

"None too soon," Dobbs said. "It's gonna snow like hell, sir."

Taylor agreed with Dobbs's observation. He had already swung his bay's head, and was already pleasantly anticipating a glass of brandy, a cup of coffee, and a warm stove, when he saw them.

"What is that, Miller?"

Miller's eyes followed the lieutenant's pointing, wavering finger. Miller squinted into the distance and saw them for himself.

A black, tiny form rolling northward across the plains, another smaller form beside it. "Looks like a man leading an ox wagon, sir."

Dobbs swallowed a curse. That meant they were going to be a while getting to Number Nine. Taylor himself sighed. "Let's welcome them to Wyoming," he said, glancing again at the northern skies, where the wall of unnatural blue still progressed southward. A granddaddy of a blue norther was fixing to blow, and they couldn't be in a worse position, exposed as they were.

Taylor buttoned the top button on his greatcoat and turned

his collar to the wind. They rode southward then, toward the tiny, distant wagon and the incredibly small figure of a man who walked beside it.

Behind them the massive wall of weather mounted ominously higher and darker; the grass before them trembled in the wind.

Before they reached the wagon, the first snow had begun to fall.

EASY COMPANY

Ride the High Plains with the rough-and-tumble Infantrymen of
Outpost Nine—in John Wesley Howard's EASY COMPANY series!

LONGARM

_____	06515-5 LONGARM #1	$2.25
_____	05899-8 LONGARM AND THE AVENGING ANGELS #3	$1.95
_____	06063-1 LONGARM IN THE INDIAN NATION #5	$1.95
_____	05900-5 LONGARM AND THE LOGGERS #6	$1.95
_____	05901-3 LONGARM AND THE HIGHGRADERS #7	$1.95
_____	05985-4 LONGARM AND THE NESTERS #8	$1.95
_____	05973-0 LONGARM AND THE HATCHET MAN #9	$1.95
_____	06064-X LONGARM AND THE MOLLY MAGUIRES #10	$1.95
_____	06626-5 LONGARM AND THE TEXAS RANGERS #11	$2.25
_____	05903-X LONGARM IN LINCOLN COUNTY #12	$1.95
_____	06153-0 LONGARM IN THE SAND HILLS #13	$1.95
_____	06070-4 LONGARM IN LEADVILLE #14	$1.95
_____	05904-8 LONGARM ON THE DEVIL'S TRAIL #151	$1.95
_____	06104-2 LONGARM AND THE MOUNTIES #16	$1.95
_____	06154-9 LONGARM AND THE BANDIT QUEEN #17	$1.95
_____	06155-7 LONGARM ON THE YELLOWSTONE #18	$1.95
_____	05905-6 LONGARM IN THE FOUR COURNERS #19	$1.95